Crossings

Ashley Capes

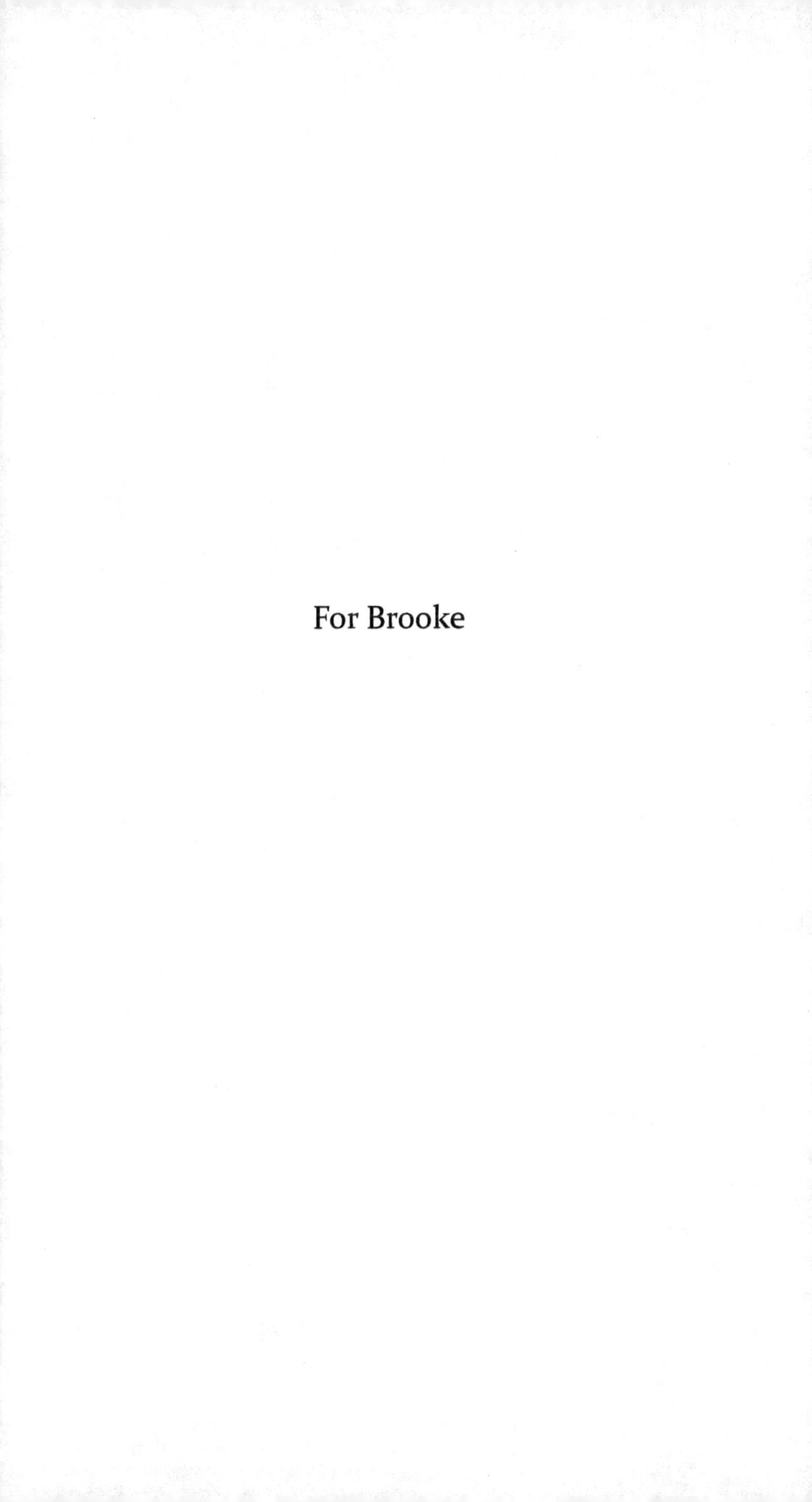

For Brooke

Chapter 1.

Lisa crouched by the tracks, frowning at the scuff marks as she brushed pale eucalypt leaves from gouges in the dirt. No bigger than a typical roo at a guess; what was old Pumps on about? A giant white kangaroo? Sounded like a myth. Maybe one in twenty thousand roos were albino, but no kangaroo stood three metres tall. She wiped sweat from her face; even in the shade it had to be over thirty. More likely his eyes had failed him. Or the farmer was just after attention. Ever since his wife died, he could talk the legs off a chair.

She looked up at Pumps, who leant on his shovel, scratching at grey stubble. "What do you think then? Am I right? She's big, isn't she? I'll be in the bloody Guinness Book of Records soon."

"Hard to say, Mr Johnson. The tracks aren't clear – the ground's too hard."

"Come on, give it a chance. I saw what I saw."

"A bone-white roo heading into the trees, bigger than a

horse?"

"Right."

"Ah, what did it do?"

He pointed to the treeline, the messmate with its grey bark like corduroy, packed close to the fence. "She came down and must've kicked over the fence there. She was sniffing around. I was coming up around the shed; didn't see her at first."

Lisa nodded. Something *had* broken the fence, knocking two posts down and snapping the wire. The big shed, its corrugated iron rusted, stood beside an old tractor whose giant wheels were sinking into the grass. It was pretty far away and Pumps had to be in his seventies – were his eyes that good?

"Could have been kids or a tourist got lost and they broke the fence," Lisa suggested.

"No tyre tracks."

She nodded. Stupid. Of course. "Sure it wasn't smaller?"

"Damn it, I'm not blind yet, Lisa. It was big. Too big. And that's just the body. Standing straight she would have been four metres easy."

Even two metres for a big, adult eastern grey was an upper limit, but Pumps was convinced so she didn't argue. "Did you follow her?"

He grumbled. "Wanted to but my hip's acting up."

"Well, it won't hurt for me to have a look, I guess," she said.

"That's what I said on the phone, girl."

Girl? Granted, she wasn't an old timer but she was hardly a 'girl' either. Lisa sighed; it didn't really matter. "I'll let you know what I find." She stepped over the fence and ducked into the shrub, her Lidelson Wildlife shirt snagging on a branch, right at the paw print logo. She unhooked it and turned back to Pumps, who'd resumed hacking the earth. If his eyes were shot at least his body didn't appear to be wearing out – he'd finish his new fence in no time at that rate.

Her boots crunched over leaves and twigs as she ducked and weaved between branches. There were no animal trails and not a lot of open space. A kangaroo as big as Pumps described would have a tight squeeze. She slipped between a pair of gums and pushed through a screen of leaves, the scent of eucalypt strong in the air.

The thud of Pumps' shovel dulled as she moved deeper, finally pausing at an old trail. Its edges were overgrown and a fallen log crossed it – its surface thick with moss. Droppings lay at its base, not unlike a small pile of coal.

Only it wasn't small. It was enough for three kangaroos.

The droppings were days old now and Pumps called this morning. By themselves they didn't prove anything. Lisa climbed the log, heading along the trail, eyes roving the bush. The call of magpies echoed and she waved away a fly.

Still no real signs of the mysterious giant... "Wait a minute," she murmured.

A tuft of fur lay pressed against the base of a big messmate. She strode over and plucked it free; it was coarse beneath her finger and thumb. Pale but not truly white. It could have been from a regular-sized kangaroo, or even a wombat.

Lisa pocketed the fur and completed a circle of the tree. Something had happened around it though, maybe a fight? Or a kill. The ground was torn, deep gouges and scuffmarks scattering decaying leaves. But there was no blood or other fur. Just a mess of earth and no clues as to why.

She started back and by the time she emerged, Pumps had paused to drink from a bottle, shovel driven into the earth beside him. He was sitting on an old stump but stood when he saw her. "Anything?"

"Not really." She showed him the fur. "I found this but it's not much."

His eyes lit up when he saw it. "Gotta be proof, don't it?"

"I'm not sure; it might not even be kangaroo. And it looks grey to me."

He frowned. "But you'd know, wouldn't you?"

"Well, it probably *is* kangaroo but most likely from an old grey."

"Looks white to me."

"How about I get it tested?" Maybe on a slow day, anyway.

"That-a girl. We'll be on the map before you know it."

Lisa laughed. "If you say so. I think I'd rather the peace and quiet."

"I hear you." His nod was approving. "But it'd be nice to have just a taste of the spotlight too."

"I did see something else."

"Yeah?"

"Did you hear anything strange, like grunting or growling? I wonder if some roos weren't fighting back there. Though they'd usually go for open spaces," she said.

"Nope, nothing like that."

She shrugged. "Well, I'll head into town now and see what I can come up with."

"Thanks for taking a look. But I haven't given up yet; I saw her."

"Maybe you should carry a camera around?"

He snapped his fingers. "Good idea."

Lisa waved as she headed back to the ute. It needed a clean; dust smothered what was once white paint. Hopping in, she shot off a text to Robert at the centre, letting him know it was all clear, then headed down the bumpy road to the highway. Green flashed by, the roar of wind burying the radio as she drove, one elbow hanging out the window.

Strands of blonde whipped at her eyes and she tucked the hair behind her ear. Should have tied it back better. She slowed for a sharp corner and a police Land Cruiser flashed its lights as she passed. Lisa waved, only a glimpse of Gerry's dark hair visible behind the wheel. Was there more trouble out at the Brown's place? Idiots were always drunk, always fighting with the neighbours about something. Last week it was Billy Brown accusing the Healys of killing one of his sheep.

The brush began to recede as homes grew up around her, their sprawling yards, winding dirt driveways and thinning trees soon giving way to sealed entryways and rows of smaller houses, all basically the same but with variation of brick or roof colour. Living in each other's pockets, Mum would have said.

She pulled into her own street of small-town architectural conformity, rolling up to her by-the-numbers two bedroom, grey roof, orange brick place and cut the engine. The ute's clock gave her a prod: quarter to five; she only had an hour to get ready for work – the glamour of being a wildlife volunteer didn't quite pay the bills.

As Lisa crossed the path to her home she stopped.

Something red lay in a heap on her doorstep. She crept closer, wrinkling her nose as the buzz of flies led her to a pile of animal entrails. Slick with blood, like mangled tubes from bike tyres, they stained the concrete.

"What the hell?"

She turned back to the street with a shudder. A kid chased a ball along the footpath but otherwise it was empty, quiet. Just the sun beating down on the road.

Who'd do such a thing?

Chapter 2.

The next day, Lisa found herself kneeling by the side of the road just out of town. An eye had been half-smeared across the road. Nestled beside pink flesh, tufts of fur and congealed blood, it was barely recognisable. The rest of the kangaroo lay twisted in a grassy ditch at the treeline, intestines in a slick trail that glistened under the noon sun. A thick stench hung over the road.

Seems there was no escaping blood and guts lately.

Last night she'd cleaned up the viscera as best she could but the stain remained on her doorstep and there was no way to know who was responsible. Probably just kids screwing around, a stupid prank. No use dwelling on it.

Lisa turned to the carcass in the ditch. Poor thing. It was common enough on Swallow's Road with all its blind corners but still... She pulled her first glove on and glanced around at the grey trunks of the messmate and the paler gums.

"Robert?"

No answer from the bush. He wasn't in the ute either. Probably relieving himself behind a tree somewhere.

At the ditch, she knelt by the body and checked the animal's pouch. Thankfully, no joey. Whoever had called in the kill had probably left the roo where it tumbled but Lisa wasn't lifting it into the ute by herself – not the largest kangaroo but still too awkward for one person to lift easily.

She turned back to the trees and shouted. "Robert, where the hell are you?"

A voice drifted back. "Coming." The crunch of branches followed and within moments Robert clambered into view, his green jacket zipped up and his broad face apologetic. "Sorry. I had to go."

"I guessed." His long trip was meant to spare her, she supposed, but probably had more to do with his need for privacy. "No joeys, so we'll take her straight to Anthony's."

He sighed. "Don't people know who to call for road-kill?"

"Maybe she was alive when they called?"

He paused. "Good point. So, did you want to drag her off to the side? Good food for scavengers." He asked his question in the tone of someone who knew the answer he was going to get.

"No, we'll take her."

"You'll owe Anthony a year's worth of diesel soon."

"I know."

"All right then."

Together they lifted the roo, and with Lisa at the tail and Robert grimacing when he gripped the bloodiest end of the body, walked to the ute where they placed the kangaroo into the tray. Working quickly, she tied the roo down with rope taken from the toolbox then hesitated.

"I'll just be a minute, Robert."

"Last rites?" he said.

"Yeah."

He nodded and busied himself disposing of bloody gloves before hopping into the cab. Lisa peeled off her own gloves then removed a small bag from her jacket. From within she took a large pinch of salt, sprinkling it over the body. The tiny white grains slipped between the fur. "Watch over her," she said.

To who, it didn't matter; only that she said it.

Jumping into the cab, she fired the engine and switched the radio off, falling into the rhythm of easing off before corners, accelerating out again. A little way down the road Robert glanced at her.

"What is it?" She didn't take her eyes from the black strip of road cutting through the green.

"Why do you always do that?"

"No-one else does."

"No, I mean, the salt, not the ritual."

She shrugged. "Dad used to do it with our pets. I guess I just got it from him."

"Oh." He reached for the cup holder, sipping the juice. "How is he?"

"The same." Lisa kept her voice even.

"Sorry."

"It's not your fault."

They drove on in silence, her hands tight on the wheel and him drinking his orange juice. After about the fortieth sip, she had to laugh.

"I'm going to have to pull over soon, aren't I?"

He blinked. "What? Why?"

She laughed again. "All that juice."

"Yes ma'am, point taken." He lowered the bottle. "I meant

to ask you before; what did old Pumps have to say? Did he really believe he saw a giant kangaroo?"

"He thinks he's going to be in the Guinness Book of World Records."

"Right."

"I have some fur but I think it's from a grey. There might have been something fighting on his property, but."

"Well, I won't hold my breath for another appearance of his mystery roo."

The trees soon began to thin as they neared town. A wooden sign sat right beside the road. Painted brown, its white letters were filled with lichen but still managed to spell out 'Lidelson.' The claim of being a 'Gateway to the Alpine Region' was less fortunate, having long since been swallowed but for the tips of the capital letters.

Anthony's clinic waited just on the edge of the town proper, appearing after a long bend in the road lined by young gums. The building was wide, its peaked roof dotted with solar panels and its windows flashed sunlight as they pulled up around back.

Half-concealed by green Banksia flowers that lined the rear of the property was the incinerator. Dark and large as a truck trailer with a chimney, it lay silent for now, but wouldn't stay quiet for long. Lisa hopped out of the ute and knocked on the back door while Robert worked on the ties.

Anthony answered. Dressed in a white smock with gloves hanging out of a pocket, the vet had impeccably groomed silver hair. He chewed on a sandwich. "Lisa." He glanced over at the ute. "Got another one?"

"Roo today. She had no joeys at least."

"Well, your timing's good. I've got a cremation later on,

feel free to add your roo."

"Thanks, Anthony." He was a good guy. Usually only city vets incinerated road-kill but Anthony had always indulged her – animals deserved dignity in death. And she knew the council-practice of leaving road-kill to feed other animals was all part of the cycle of life and death. She knew it. Knew it a hundred times over but still...there was something cold about just leaving them there... Maybe she would buy some fuel for Anthony next time.

"You got any more calls today?" Anthony asked.

"Not yet. Gonna try have lunch back at the office for a change."

Anthony grinned. "It's not that good – someone always interrupts."

"Very funny." She smiled back. "We'll get going then."

He waved as he stepped back inside.

Lisa returned to the ute, where she helped Robert carry the body to the bulky incinerator. The roo slumped into the dark hollow with a thud. Better than the side of the road at least. She sighed, signalling to Robert. "Let's go then."

"Want me to drive?" he asked, wiping his hands on his pants.

"I'm fine. Besides, you're a little slow and I'm hungry."

He snorted as she took the driver's seat, woke the engine and pulled around the front of the building. She flicked the indicator on at the turn and waited, glancing at the empty road. One of the guideposts was missing its red reflector. Maybe lunch at the centre was a bad idea. Dad hadn't called today. Was he all right? Damn it, if he'd fallen again or even if –

"Lisa?"

She blinked. "Huh?"

"You right? There's no-one coming."

"Right." She pulled onto the highway and headed for the town centre. Traffic slowed them when they passed the quiet supermarket, and she stared into an interstate numberplate – one of the old yellow ones.

"Take Foster Street," Robert said. "You can skip the light."

She glanced at him. "You mean Lidelson's single traffic light?"

"It bugs me," he said with a shrug.

Lisa obliged, turning into the narrow street and pulling into the Wildlife Station mere moments sooner than they would have otherwise. Robert appeared pleased so she didn't say anything, though she hid a smile.

A little Honda waited in the shade of the earthen car park and a woman paced before the locked office. Her handbag hung from a low branch of the gum that spread its canopy over the roof of the small building. Lisa squinted – it looked like Steph – was she okay? Her blonde curls bounced as she approached, feet crunching on gravel set between wide paving slabs.

"Lisa, good," Steph said when she reached them. Her face was worried. "I didn't think you'd ever be back. I saw your sign so I waited."

"What's wrong?" she asked. The 'Back at 2pm' sign rested against the glass, right beneath the Wildlife paw-print logo and phone number. Maybe they were a little late after all.

"It's Ben; he's back."

A chill ran through her blood.

No. It'd been years. He'd moved away. Things had been better. Lisa felt her hand drift to a long scar inside her forearm, as if moving of its own volition. "What did he want?"

Steph took her hand, the warmth welcome. "I was at the bank – he's buying a house and moving back. Apparently he made some money in real estate." She lowered her voice. "He said he wants to see you."

No way was that going to happen. "Fat chance."

Steph kissed Lisa's cheek. "Good girl. I just wanted to give you a heads up. I have to get back to the cafe."

"Thanks."

"Call me if you need," she called over her shoulder as she strode to her car.

Lisa made for the office, jamming her keys into the lock. That bastard. He had no right to come back. To *her* town. Shit. Had Ben left the animal entrails on her front step? Shit. She flung the door open and snatched the sign from the window, tossing it behind the counter.

"Is something wrong? Who's Ben?" Robert asked when he caught up.

"My ex," she said, following the sign to rummage around in the backroom. "I just need a minute, Robert." She found her bag and went out back, fumbling with a lighter and a crumpled pack of 25s. She ripped one out.

"Shit." She paced beneath ferns, cigarette in hand. A huge terracotta pot sat near the door – empty of plants but instead, in black dirt, pale orange butts sat like dead worms.

Robert appeared at the screen door, eyebrow raised. "That bad?"

"Don't tell me," she said.

"Tell you what?"

"That I shouldn't smoke." She put the cigarette back and

jammed the pack into her bag. "Because I know that."

He raised his hands. "I wasn't going to say anything." He frowned as he leaned against the doorframe. "What's wrong? What's the go with your ex?"

She stared at Robert a moment. He was new – relatively – only having volunteered for a few months now. The other guys, Sally and Colin, they remembered Ben. Five years he'd been gone, and now he was back and asking after her. Lisa exhaled. Did Robert really need to hear about more of her problems? Was he at risk of being drawn in to them?

Lisa took a breath; he'd find out soon enough. "Ben's a controlling scum-bag that used to hit me."

"Seriously? I'm sorry."

"Don't be sorry, it's fine. I got out." She kicked the terracotta. "God knows what he wants now, though."

"So what are you going to do?"

"Ignore him."

"What if he drops around?"

"I'll tell him to fuck off."

Robert's mouth hung open a moment before a laugh escaped. "I don't think I've ever heard you say that."

She had to grin. "I usually keep it to myself."

"So what now?"

"Do you mind covering for me? I want to go and check on Dad."

"No probs."

"Thanks. And if Ben turns up, tell him I'm done for the day."

Chapter 3.

Lisa crossed the verandah of the old weatherboard house, stepping over the squeaky board and pausing at the door to rub her temples. The chatter of the radio drifted through open curtains. Horse scratchings; he was listening to the races.

The right key came easily to hand but she didn't open the door.

Please be okay, Dad.

A breeze rustled elm leaves in the driveway and chimes tinkled. The wind picked up, buffeting her back. It brought the smell of charred leaves with it – someone burning-off in preparation for fire-season, no doubt. "All right then," she told the wind.

Lisa turned the key and stepped inside.

Her father sat, perched on the edge of a faded green armchair. Dressed in brown slacks and white shirt, he faced the old radio with its big silver dial. He had a pen and newspaper in hand but didn't write. Embers glowed in the fireplace despite the summer heat. A row of pictures lined the mantle – she couldn't stop a smile; they ought to have melted by now.

"Hush, Annie," he said, without looking from the radio. Damn.

Lisa closed her eyes as she rested her bag on the table, but soon went for a glass of water from the kitchen. She drank while the scratchings finished. Best to wait – even when he was well; he never heard a thing she said when the scratchings were on.

She joined him, crouching by the chair. "Dad, it's me, Lisa."

He blinked at her. "Lisa? Oh, when did you get here?"

"Just now."

He turned to the door. "I thought Annie just..."

"Dad, Mum's been gone for a long time now."

Her father said nothing.

She took his hand. "Have you eaten?"

Now he snorted but his smile was warm. "Of course I have, don't be daft, sweetheart."

"What did you have?"

"What?"

"To eat."

He ran his free hand through white hair as he stood, moving to the table to spread the newspaper. Checking on the next race no doubt. "Ham and cheese sandwiches."

"Yeah?"

"Don't believe me?" He laughed. "Want me to open my guts?"

She shook her head – trying to stop another smile. He was so close to being his usual self, but she had to be sure. "I'm going to check, I don't want you skipping meals."

"Go for your life."

She opened the fridge and drew out a block of cheese. Sealed. "Dad, didn't I buy this for you yesterday?"

"Maybe. Guess I finished the last of the other block." He frowned, mouth twitching as confusion passed over his face. But he glanced at the radio; a race had just begun. "I better keep an eye on that."

"I'll make you something for later, then."

He nodded and Lisa let him go, replacing the cheese before moving to the study. A few bills lay on the heavy desk – unopened and unpaid. She sat down on the hard chair, drew out his chequebook from a drawer and got to work.

*

Back home, Lisa flicked on a lamp and moved through the yellow light. It fell across paintings lining the walls, half of them painted by Dad. She paused before one, raising a hand to hover before the ridges in the paint. A brilliant purple butterfly was bursting from a cocoon – the first in his series actually hung in her study, a red caterpillar cloaked in its wrapping. She forced back a lump in her throat, then moved to close the blinds.

Finally, she slumped into her own armchair – the twin of Dad's – and sighed.

Tea with Dad wasn't too good; mumbled responses as he stared at the television. The clink of cutlery on plates. Trying not to let him see her watching him. At least he stayed in the present for the rest of the evening.

"Chin up," she muttered. A bitter laugh followed. What a stupid saying – as if lifting her chin would change anything.

He was getting worse and she couldn't help. Couldn't stop it, couldn't do a fucking thing. Maybe it was time for the doctor, to get him checked for dementia. She had to talk to him about it next time, no more putting it off.

Headlights flashed beyond the curtains.

Lisa straightened in the chair. Who was visiting so late? Steph with more news? Or was it Ben? Had he found her new place? She stood and rattled the door handle. Locked. Good. And the curtains were drawn – but with the crunch of feet on the stone walkway, it was probably too late to hit the lamp and pretend no-one was home.

The footsteps stopped at the door.

Hard raps on wood followed.

She kept still, holding her breath. If it was him...

More knocking. "Lisa, it's Ben."

Go away.

He stopped and his sigh cut through the night. "I know you don't want to see me, but I'm not leaving until we talk. That's all I want."

She shook her head; he'd tried that one before. The memory of a deep bruise tingled on her upper arm, then her leg and her ribs – there weren't many places he hadn't hurt her.

"Please. We owe each other."

Lisa folded her arms, even though he couldn't see. Her jaw was clenched.

"Fine, I'll sleep out here and we can talk in the morning." His tone straddled anger and coercion.

"Piss off, Ben."

"I knew you were home," he said, and she could hear the smirk in his voice. "Come on, can't we talk?" The handle jiggled and she flinched.

She stamped a foot – at herself as much as him. It was locked, he wasn't getting in. "No."

"Now you're being childish."

She slipped across the room and grabbed her mobile. "Ben, I don't want to see you. Get off my front step."

"This is bullshit, Lisa. How can I make amends if you won't let me in?"

She clenched her teeth. Prick. Who did he think he was fooling? "You can't. And why do you think I care after five years? After what you did?"

He raised his voice. "I'm serious. Let me in."

That was too much. She strode back to the door, body trembling. Adrenaline or fear? Didn't matter. "No – and that's the end of it. Unless you want to kick the door in and hit me again. You still like that, right?"

He swore and his footsteps crunched away, followed by the slam of a car door.

Not until his engine faded did she move back to the chair and collapse. Her pulse was racing. She rested her mobile on the soft fabric of the arm, the shaking of her hand almost knocking the phone to the floor.

Holy shit. Shouldn't have provoked him. Had she pushed too far?

He could have broken in and then who knows what would have happened? No. She wasn't a victim. But she *was* a realist. She dialled Steph's number. "Steph, I'm sorry to wake you – but can you come over? I need you."

"What's wrong, honey?"

"Ben was here."

Steph's voice hardened. "I'll be there."

Lisa paced the dim lounge until someone knocked on the front door. "Steph?"

"Let me in, it's cold out here."

Lisa opened the door. "It's summer – it's not even..." she trailed off. Steph wore striped pyjamas beneath a fuzzy blue dressing gown but other details were fleeting. Her friend held a splitter. It looked to have been wrenched from the chopping block moments before she arrived – a splinter fell to the lino when she rested it against the wall.

"What's that?"

Steph pointed a finger at her. "For you, for tonight. If he comes back."

"I'm not going to murder him."

"I just want you to feel safe."

She shook her head, but already tension melted from her shoulders. It was good to see Steph, even if she was overreacting. Probably. "I have kitchen knives, you know."

"Then go get one and put it near the bed."

"Isn't that a bit much? He won't be back."

Her mouth spread into a thin line. "I know what he's capable of. Remember the last time?"

Lisa frowned. Her forefingers strayed back to the surgical scar beneath her forearm. Which 'last' time? Time he put her in hospital? Or, when he 'only' broke her arm. Or maybe when he accidently killed their cat.

Or so he claimed at the time. And she'd wondered about that. He could be so, so petty.

"Well? I took you to the hospital myself, remember? I know what he's like."

"Sorry, yeah. All right." Lisa looked to the lamp, the front door, anywhere but her friend's expression. "I'll make up the spare bed."

*

She woke to a sound outside her window. Moonlight exhaled through a slice in the curtains. She held her breath. From the spare room came the faint grinding of Steph snoring and the subtle hum of the fridge slipped out of the kitchen, but no new noises from outside.

What had it been? A scrape of something against the wall? A thump? Had something hit the glass?

She peeled back the sheet. The rustle of cloth against cloth was a storm.

Her bare feet sunk a fraction into the carpet as she crept to the window. If she opened it, would there be something waiting? What if Ben was back? She made a fist. That piece of shit! Lisa leant to take the kitchen knife from her bedside table. Her hand shook but she ground her teeth.

None of that.

With her free hand she reached out to pull the curtain open.

Nothing.

Only moonlight spilling across the backyard lawn. The clothesline stood at the end of a concrete path, unmoving. Garden boxes lined the fence. Up the back, the big elm was silent. Nothing amiss.

Lisa sunk back to the bed and waited.

She'd imagined it. Dreamt it maybe. Lisa put the knife down and slipped beneath the sheet. Only the passage of her breathing, hum of the fridge and Steph's snoring, still faint.

Try and relax.

It was nothing.

Lisa pulled her knees up and stared at the window.

Chapter 4.

"Lisa, wake up."

Lisa blinked as Steph's curls and wide eyes resolved from the shadows. Golden sunlight singed the edges of her hair.

"What's wrong?" She frowned, casting a quick glance at the open curtains – nothing but green leaves and blue sky.

"You're out of bin liners and I'm making us eggs for breakfast and so I went to take some rubbish out to the recycle bin and there's something there." Her words ran together. "You have to see it."

Lisa threw back warm sheets. "Is it Ben?"

"No, just come on." Steph pulled her out of bed. Lisa stumbled after, nearly smacking into the dresser on the way out and then dodging a hall table, bare feet slapping on the floorboards.

"Wait, let me put some shoes on," she said. "And a top or something." All she wore was shorts and a thin singlet, not really an outdoors outfit. She found an old t-shirt and dragged it over her head while Steph waited by the front door, tapping a foot.

"All right." Lisa stepped into a pair of thongs.

"I think it's dead," Steph said as she opened the door and pointed.

Lisa paused on the doorstep. "Is that..." A kangaroo lay across her front path, a tuft of fur stirring in a soft breeze. She dashed over, kneeling on the grass. Its fur was grey and *white*, mottled. Not like a regular wallaby – this was a big eastern grey. Only it was pale, even its cracked claws were without colour. The empty eyes were clouded with cataracts and its whiskers were long and white too, she'd never seen a roo so old.

Was this the kangaroo Pumps Johnson had seen?

It was hardly a giant. And not albino either – just... ancient.

Why had it chosen her front yard as a final resting place, rather than stay in the wild? Or, had someone dumped it here?

"It's dead, isn't it?" Steph called from the door.

"Yeah." She stood with a sigh. "Can you bring me some salt?"

"Your thing?" There was no judgement in her voice – Steph had seen the ritual often enough, the first time was probably the family dog, Patch. The old blue heeler had died in his sleep back when they were still girls, after a sleepover.

Dad had taken them to the backyard to explain what happened and then produced some salt, letting it trickle from a big, calloused hand. It fell into Patch's fur. When she'd asked why, he put the other hand on her shoulder. "Tradition. My father taught me, and his father taught him and now you can do as we have. Make sure you ask that someone looks after him too," he'd said.

Lisa gave Steph a nod. "Yeah, my thing."

When Steph returned with salt she tiptoed over, stretching her arm across the path. Lisa took the shaker. "You the same girl who brought an axe over for me to use on my ex?"

"It's not funny. I don't like dead animals, you know that."

"It's okay." Lisa bent down, twisted the shaker into her palm then sprinkled some salt into the fur. "Watch over him." She removed her phone and took a photo to show Pumps – keeping the roo's eyes out of shot. It didn't seem right to photograph him, like he was a trophy, or a 'kill'.

"I better call the centre then."

"Great idea." Steph led the way back inside.

Once dressed properly, Lisa called the office and got a hold of Robert, explaining what had happened. "Be there soon," he said.

Lisa ate her eggs with Steph while she waited. "Thanks for coming over last night." She took another mouthful – good stuff; Steph had mixed cheese and pepper into the scramble. "Something else happened, but I didn't mention it and I feel silly now though. Light of day and all that."

"Don't. I'm happy to help." She set a coffee mug down. "Tell me."

"I found a heap of entrails on my front step the other day."

Steph's eyes grew wide. "What? I didn't see anything in the dark – that's sick."

"Yeah. So what do you think?"

"You mean Ben?" She frowned. "Doesn't make sense. The timing might be right, but it's hardly the way to win you back."

"I know. But maybe he's trying to get me off-balance. Make me feel vulnerable. Swoop in as the hero."

"Didn't think he was that smart," Steph said.

"Me either."

"And the kangaroo? Do you think that was him too?"

"Maybe." She wasn't going to ask him.

"So what's next?"

"I'm going to the station."

Steph took her plate to the sink. "You hoping your boyfriend Gerry will be there?"

"Very funny."

"Come on, I reckon he likes you," Steph said with a grin.

"Do you just?"

"Yes. Since school."

"What?"

Steph chuckled as she rinsed her plate. "He couldn't do anything because of Ben. And we'd have freaked out; called him a cradle-snatcher or something."

"He was only two years ahead of us."

"Making excuses for him now, huh?"

Lisa put her fork down. "Want me to go get the kangaroo? Bring it in and put it up here with us so it can share my eggs?"

Steph laughed. "All right, I'll shut up. But I don't know why you don't go for him."

"Look, I'm just going to report the entrails and maybe Gerry will go and speak to Ben, okay? Is he staying with his parents?"

She shrugged. "He didn't say. Let me know how it goes with Gerry – I have to get going. Dave's probably making a mess in the kitchen without me."

"He's not that bad."

"Yes, he is." Steph gave her a peck on the cheek. "Be careful – I'm taking the splitter home so find yourself a good axe, will you?"

She had to laugh. "I'll think about it."

Lisa walked Steph to her car and waved her off from the front step. Before she could head back indoors, the white shape of the Wildlife Centre ute pulled into her driveway. Robert hopped out. "Morning."

"Hi, Robert."

He snapped gloves on as he crossed the lawn. "He is old."

"I know. Must have really pushed the limits."

"Don't get angry, but you know this is another job we might have given to the shire." He held up his hands. "I don't mind, but I'm just saying."

"I know – but they send enough our way, I'm just saving them a phone call." She grinned. "And you must be getting used to me by now, right?"

"Yeah, I guess I am," he said with a smile. "Well, let's load the old fella up."

Lisa helped Robert lift the kangaroo into the ute. She stroked the fur a moment, then stepped back. Robert had paused, resting his forearms on the tray. "It's strange, isn't it? Why did he come into town?"

"Don't know. Maybe I'll mention it to Pumps." No need to point the finger at Ben just yet – at least not with Robert. Probably better to keep him out of it.

Robert found his keys. "He'll be disappointed if this is his roo."

"True. But he'll get over it."

Once Robert left, she grabbed her bag from the house before locking up and heading to her own car – a red and silver '87 Commodore. It wasn't much cleaner than the ute and it was getting old too – the rubber of the steering wheel had long since started crumbling away after decades of harsh summers, but it started every time.

She drove over to the police station with the window down. The building was a squat, square thing with a blue stripe for a roof, without an air-conditioner it would have been a hot box of trapped air. Easy to imagine it sweating rivets.

The squad car was parked out front. She pulled in behind it and headed up the path. Gerry exited before she reached the door, hat in hand, wiping crumbs from his blue shirt. Muscles strained beneath the light blue fabric and she smiled. Why didn't he just buy the next size up? Gerry the Gym-Junkie.

"Hi Lisa, how are you? How's your dad?"

"Actually, I'm a bit worried." She glanced at the car; Karen must have had the 4-wheel drive. "Are you on your way out?"

"Just following-up with the Brown boy." He rubbed his cheek, clean-shaven. "Rang through another complaint about dead sheep – two this time. What's wrong?"

"A couple of things, actually. Ben's back."

His expression darkened. "Has he been to see you?"

"Yeah, but I didn't let him in. He stormed off."

"Look, we can do the paperwork for an intervention order right now –"

"It's okay, he'd just ignore it, but if you could go visit him maybe? I think Ben's at his parents' place."

"Want me to send him packing again?"

"No, just let him know you're watching him."

He grinned, and she got a glimpse of the boy within the

man. "It'd be my pleasure."

"And one more thing. I don't know if it's related."

"Shoot."

"I found a pile of animal entrails on my front step the other day. Heard of anything like that around town?"

He shook his head, a frown forming. "No. Do you think Ben's behind it?"

She sighed. "I don't know."

"I'll see how he reacts when I mention it."

"Thanks, Gerry."

"No problem. Look after yourself."

She gave an assurance as she climbed back into the Holden, letting Gerry head off first. Would it make a difference? With Ben, who knew. There'd been a time when he listened. In the beginning. They'd plan for the future. Go house-hunting and make an afternoon of it, eating take-away in the car. Things were actually fun. Even something simple like seeing a movie together and laughing about it on the way out of the cinema.

He put a stop to that the first time he hit her.

Lisa headed for the pub where it lurked on a hill, overlooking the glittering river. Beautiful as it was, it was not exactly the perfect place for drunk people to stumble home from. She turned into the gravel car park. Even safer than the Tobe River flowing behind the pub were the concrete steps leading up to its verandah. How many customers had she seen fall down them in just the last year? One poor bastard, Freddie the Butcher, lost a tooth. His grin was hilarious now, but nothing was going to change – Bruce, the owner, didn't see the point.

"They keep coming back, Lisa, why bother?"

Quiet voices sifted through the frosted yellow glass in the door. She pushed it open to find Bruce and his chef, Matthew, discussing the evening menu. A thin man with midnight-black hair, Bruce's elbows jutted from his white shirt – she'd seen him knock half a dozen clean glasses from a tray with those elbows.

"Sorry I'm a bit late." She dumped her bag on the bar.

Bruce smiled. "No problems."

"Might start in the back." The pub had a few rooms for tourists, not that they were rented out much. Most people went further out bush to stay in cabins, or closer to the coast. Lidelson had a reputation as a great place to stop for lunch, but few people extended it to overnight. The rooms would make an easy start after a rough night.

"Sounds good," Bruce said.

Matthew nodded to her. "You had a visitor yesterday."

"What?"

His round face shifted into a grimace. "Real arrogant prick. Bill? No, Ben. He asked Bruce if you still worked here and didn't like it when you weren't in."

God-damn it. "Yeah, he's my ex. He can get kinda angry though, so leave him alone if he comes back."

"What's his problem?"

"He's got more than one," she said, grabbing her bag and heading through to the back. In the hall closet she wrestled the vacuum cleaner from its nest of handles and dragged it into the first bedroom – still number '4' since Bruce hadn't bothered to change it after gutting the first three rooms to make space for the pool tables.

She rammed the plug into the power point. Ben was going to be a problem. He had shit for brains if he thought he could come home and win her back. Maybe Gerry would be able to give him the hint, but the old Ben was stubborn. Was the new Ben any different? Not fucking likely. There was no new Ben. She knelt and shoved the vacuum's head beneath the bed. Each time it hit the skirting board the 'clack' gave her a scrap of satisfaction. If only it was his head.

By the time she'd done the floors, changed the sheets and given the bathroom a once over, sweat had begun to slide down her back. In the next room she put the air-con on while she worked and the rhythm of the job melted the morning away. By lunch she'd already moved on to her next client – Jacinta Ascot, who'd thankfully remembered to leave the key in her letterbox this time.

Jacinta's house was messy but not dirty. Kids' toys, newspapers, a TV guide spilling out like a red tongue from a papery spider, and clothes draped across chairs and beds; nothing that Lisa couldn't fix up in short order. She mopped the kitchen tiles then vacuumed to finish, pausing in the study. Peter, Jacinta's husband, had a stuffed fox in his study. It stood snarling at the computer desk – so he'd have his back to it while he worked.

Why did he want such a thing?

She tapped the power button with her toe and took his jacket from the back of the computer chair, draping it over the fox. "Have a rest, buddy." His frozen expression of rage – which Lisa always imagined was directed at Peter – must have been tiring. What a pose to be stuck with for eternity... or until she came again next Wednesday and covered him up for a few minutes.

Once Lisa finished, and had replaced the jacket, she packed up the vacuum cleaner and paused in the kitchen.

What if... She opened the pantry and flicked the light. There – salt and pepper. She took a pinch of salt and returned to the study and sprinkled it over the fox. "Watch over him."

Chapter 5.

No visits from Ben overnight and a cold breakfast instead of eggs the next morning. She'd dreamt of Pete's fox stealing chickens from one of the farms out of town and woke with another frown and a crick in her neck.

She flicked on the radio – scratchings for race five. "Are you getting these, Dad?" She wondered as she placed a tea bag in her cup then rubbed at her neck while it cooled. She'd have to check on him before work. There wouldn't be much time later, not while she was on call with Robert. She swiped her phone screen and hit the weather app. Thirty-five. Hot one. Should probably water the garden before it got bad. Imagine the minuscule screams the agapanthus would make if they were left to fry without a decent drink.

Lisa slipped her thongs on and slapped down the back step. At the coiled hose she stopped to gape at the yard.

Two kangaroos lay beneath the empty clothesline.

"What the hell?" She ran over and knelt, the grass scratching at her bare knees. The absolute stillness of death radiated from the bodies. Lying beside each other, their limbs and tails appeared arranged. Two more eastern greys, both male, though neither were old.

But one was missing its forepaws.

No other visible wounds on the bodies. No fur loss, no discolouration of the eyes, no discharge from the nose. She peeled open one of their mouths. No blood in the teeth either. No obvious signs of disease – not that she could be sure.

"What's happening?" She looked around, as if someone could tell her.

How had they died? Why cut off the paws? Who killed them? And, just as importantly, why here? Was it really Ben? She didn't have any other suspects.

Unless it was a joke – a really shitty, sick joke.

And would Ben really do something like that? Years ago, it would have been too much effort for him. He used to hunt but she agreed with Steph, psychological torture wasn't his thing. He preferred to use his knuckles.

Lisa ran back inside, washed her hands then grabbed her phone to call the centre.

"Lidelson Wildlife Rescue, Sally speaking."

"Sal, it's Lisa – I need a pick up."

"Lisa, hi. I didn't think you were on until later."

"I'm at home, actually."

"Yeah, heard about that – Robert told me yesterday. You don't have another one do you?"

"Two."

"Jesus, what's going on over there?"

"I wish I knew," she said.

"Well, give the next one to the council, will you? They'll

start to feel left out," Sally said.

"I'll try."

"All right then. Don't let them go anywhere."

Lisa snorted as she went to the kitchen table and emptied some salt into her palm. Last rites again. How often she'd had to perform them lately.

Sally soon arrived, backing the ute down the driveway and climbing out with a shake of her head. She tugged off her wildlife centre jacket. Fading tattoos crawled up her arms – one was a skull wrapped in a rose. "It's already too hot," she said.

Lisa nodded as she led Sally to the bodies. "Look at the paws on that one. Any ideas?"

Sally exhaled, examining each kangaroo. "Not another mark on them. It doesn't make much sense. Roos don't exactly look for backyards to die in."

"Exactly. And now three of them here." She frowned. "It's getting weird."

"Have you talked to your neighbours?"

"Not yet."

"See what they say, I guess." Sally pulled on a pair of gloves taken from her belt. "Well, let's load them up. And give me a call if you figure this out – I might actually talk to the shire about it after I take them by Anthony's. Someone might be baiting them."

"Good idea."

Lisa helped load the roos into the tray then sent Sally off to the vet. Maybe Anthony would find something.

Next door, Mr Graeme was out and on the other side Mrs Anderson hadn't seen a thing.

"Sorry dear, nothing like that." She removed her glasses

and gave them a wipe with the hem of her floral dress. "But I'll be looking from now on, you can count on me."

"Thank you." Lisa went back inside and switched her thongs for socks and shoes, despite the heat, and headed for Ronald Street, its rows of Banksia and Dad. Green now, they'd be red come autumn – his favourite season.

She pulled up and squeaked over the verandah, the wind chimes silent, and slipped inside. He was pacing the lounge room in dress shoes, slacks and shirt, suit jacket over his arm. He looked up when she opened the door, smiling as he spread his arms.

"This is a surprise."

She hugged him. The familiar scent of English Leather; he'd obviously shaved earlier. "Hi, Dad. Where are you off to?"

"Been out already, actually. I went to the post office. Had to send a letter to your Aunt Olivia. She's got that operation coming up, remember?"

Good, only the post office. Thank God he no longer drove. "I remember. Hip replacement." She'd have to call Olivia and warn her – the operation was years ago. "So what else have you got planned?"

"Just a quiet one. They're playing *Lawrence of Arabia* on TV later."

"Sounds good."

"How's work? With the animals, I mean. I'm sure cleaning is just as fun as it always was."

She laughed. "It's definitely more stimulating."

He squeezed her hand. "So, why don't you do something about it? Go back to school. You've got the brains. You'd be a wonderful vet."

"I can't afford it, Dad."

"Find a way, love."

"Maybe. If I can save enough by the end of the year." She shrugged. "Can I get a drink?"

"Help yourself." He sat, bending to untie his shoes. "And think about it," he called.

"I am."

In the kitchen she took a glass from a cupboard – the brown, fake-wood grain veneer was curling up a little at the corner – and held it under the water. Maybe now was the time to ask about getting help; be it medication or... something else. Aside from the letter, he was very much in the present, even if she'd been having the same discussion about becoming a vet since before his slide.

She had to bring it up at the right time. Her grip tightened on the glass. Maybe 'right times' were going to become rare before too long?

Footsteps squeaked outside and a knock followed.

"Mr Thomas? Are you home?"

Wait, that voice –

"Just a minute." Her dad groaned as he pulled himself up from the couch. She waved to him from the kitchen, keeping out of sight of the front window where it sliced its way down the wall beside the door.

She put a finger against her lips. "Dad, I don't want to talk to this guy, all right?"

He frowned. "Do you know him?"

"He's an ex."

"Which one?"

"Doesn't matter – can you get rid of him?"

He patted her hand. "Don't worry."

She bit her lip as he shuffled to the front door. What if Ben didn't believe him? What if he turned violent? She inched a kitchen drawer open.

"Hello?"

"Mr Thomas?"

"Yes? Can I help you?"

Ben's voice grew confused. "It's me, Ben. I used to date your daughter. I saw her car here."

"Sorry, lad. She's not in."

Lisa lifted the mallet, not just a wooden one, but an old, heavy steel beast with triangular peaks used for beating meat.

"Oh. So that's not her car?"

"It's her car but she's using my truck today." Her father's voice hardened. "What did you say your name was?"

"Ben Drummond. Can you tell her I called round, Mr Thomas?"

"I can." A pause. "Need something else?"

She peered around the edge of the wall, using the hall plant for a screen. Ben stood in the doorway, obscured by her father's arm, which barred entry to the old house. He was the same: blond hair cut close, stubble, confident – a nice smile too. Bastard. But a pink scar ran down his cheek – that was new. Who'd he pick a fight with for that one?

"No, could you just tell her that I'm staying with my parents. I haven't got her new number."

"I will."

"Thank you, Mr Thomas."

Ben left and Dad closed the door. He beamed at her. "How's that?"

Chapter 6.

Sunday morning revealed an overcast sky but, blessedly, no fresh kangaroo corpses. She had time to kill so she drove out to Pumps' farm to show him the picture of the roo. Halfway there she slowed as a log truck pulled out from a side road up ahead, momentarily blocking both lanes. She waved to the driver, who lifted a forefinger from the steering wheel as he passed.

Pumps met her by the same stretch of fencing on the edge of his yard. Light slipped between the curtains of the farmhouse and smoke smeared the sky above the chimney. Another man was making his goodbyes, climbing into a car as he did so. It looked like Frank, a neighbouring farmer. She controlled a shiver when he passed with a nod, wrinkling her nose at the stink of exhaust – or was it at Frank? The man was an amateur taxidermist. A cruel hobby.

Pumps shook his head when he saw the phone screen.

"Too small." He jerked a thumb over his shoulder. "Besides, got something else to show you. I was going to call, but you're here now."

"Something wrong?"

"Something right." He clomped over the grass to the shed. "There."

Half an entire panel looked to have been kicked in, hay peeking from a tear in the tin. Must have taken some force. "The white roo?"

"That's what I'm thinking."

"Hmmm." She circled the shed, bending low to search for white fur or tracks. She paused by the big blue tractor, dust collecting in its seat. Nothing. No signs of any animal disturbance. "I can't see any sign of her," Lisa said as she completed her circuit.

He nodded, as if he'd made the same circuit. "Heard a great thump last night. Dashed out with me torch but I was too slow. Something went crashing through the trees, though. I checked at dawn. Clear as rain."

"Over there?" Lisa turned to the treeline beyond the house.

"Reckon she leapt the fence this time."

Lisa strode over. Something was going on at Pumps' farm but a giant white kangaroo still wasn't the top of the list, was it? Just beyond the fence-line lay the wreckage of crushed bracken and snapped branches. Something *had* gone through and roughed it up.

"I'll be back," she said, bending to step through the wire.

"Take a photo if you see her," he called.

"Got my phone." She pushed into the damaged undergrowth, heading through the trees. Again, the messmate grew near enough that such a large animal would have had trouble squeezing through. At the least some fur should have rubbed off on passing but nothing. No clear tracks either. She pushed on, her pant cuffs soon damp from dew on the clinging bracken.

The deeper she went, the less signs of disturbance she saw. She'd reached about as far as she'd walked last time and nothing – all she had to show for it was a scratch on the back of her hand, a bright red stripe. Like a ghost, the damn white roo. She sighed. If the kangaroo bodies hadn't been turning up maybe she wouldn't have given Pumps' words much credence...but something odd was happening. Most likely trouble from another source.

When she returned he was standing by the stump, a mug in hand, tag from the tea-bag hanging over the side. "Anything this time?"

"No. The trail disappears back there." She paused. "Is anyone angry with you?"

Pumps gave a shrug. "Don't think so. Why?"

"Sure this isn't vandalism?"

"No, it's nothing like that, it's the roo."

"Well, maybe you should mention it to Gerry, anyway."

He chuckled. "No thanks. Don't want him coming up and scaring her off."

"But you don't think I'll scare her off?"

"I figure if anyone could manage not to, it'd be you, Lisa. You've got a way with animals, I suppose. Respect and all that."

She smiled at the old man. "Thank you."

He grinned. "Just remember, if you see something, I'm the one that saw her first, right?"

"For the Book."

"Spot on." He heaved a sigh. "Better get back to it then."

"Me too." She patted Pumps on the shoulder then returned to the Holden and headed into town.

Pulling up at Lidelson General Store, a sandwich chalkboard stood out front – the message today was courtesy of the CFA – 'Be Fire Ready'. Good, a reminder about bushfires; the perfect way to ruin a summer's day.

But then, safe was safe. Wasn't their fault.

Dad had always said, better to prepare for the worst and be relieved when it never happened. And back when he'd volunteered at the fire station, he'd seen enough to know when to prepare for trouble. She'd have to check his gutters soon.

It was cooler inside the store, between the tall shelves lined with bright packets and cans. Somewhere nearby a child wheedled with her parent, desperate for Sherbet Bombs. Lisa smiled; Sherbet Bombs had been pretty good as a kid. Not so great on the teeth, though.

"Lisa?"

Ben stood in the aisle.

He wore a plain black polo shirt and jeans, arms laden with chips, soft drink and pretzels. His Southern Cross tattoo peeked beneath the sleeve of his shirt, the outline of the bottom star. Two friends hovered nearby, talking but obviously trying not to listen. Steve and...Fathead was the other guy's nickname.

They barely registered.

"It's good to actually see you," he said with a smile. "You look good."

"What do you want?" She kept her voice even, despite the tension in her shoulders.

"Just a chance to talk."

"No screaming this time?"

He didn't take the bait. "No. I'm sorry about that. Just talk. Maybe over lunch? I'm buying a house here and I want to apologise properly."

Lisa hesitated. There *were* things she wanted to hear from him – a real apology for one. And there were things she wanted to tell him. What he'd done, how hard it had been to get her confidence back – even with help – but mostly she wanted him to know she had moved on. That her life was better; that – in the end, he'd meant nothing.

She didn't need a meal for that. "I don't think so, Ben."

He nodded. Was that a flicker of regret that he smothered? "I understand. It's not like I deserve it. Well, see you round, then." Ben turned to his friends and she heard him dump his junk food on the counter, pay and leave.

Lisa stared after him. That wasn't like Ben at all. Either he'd matured and stopped drinking – or worse, he was playing a game. A new game. His apologies always sounded sincere in the past but there had always been an element of blame-shifting. She'd made him angry. He was too drunk. A bad day at work. Getting knocked back for the house-loan.

She shuddered; this new Ben was somehow worse because he seemed reasonable, as if he were nearly ready to take responsibility for his actions, if only she gave him the chance to do so by listening. It wasn't right. He wasn't Ben; it was as if someone else were operating his body, feeding him lines, keeping his cool.

"Not falling for it, buddy." She collected what she needed from the store and fixed up Mrs Lowell before heading home, where she pulled together a bag of snacks, water and a book then jumped back into the Holden.

Maybe she could visit Dad then slip down to the coast and relax for the afternoon. West Beach wasn't too far, just an hour. It'd be nice to get out of town for a bit, to forget about Ben and white kangaroos. Or dead ones.

Lisa grabbed a jacket from a hook in the entryway and opened the door.

A pile of dead mice lay on her step.

"Again?" She dumped her bag and dashed into the street. No-one. They had to be close. The mice weren't there when she walked in and she'd not been inside that long. Lisa shielded her eyes against the rising sun but as before, all was quiet. Just the buzz of blowflies. A silver sedan pulled out of the street but nothing else.

"Fine." She went back inside, grabbed her bag, locked up and hopped back into the Holden, heading for the station. Maybe Gerry would have some news. And if Gerry had found it *was* Ben trying to mess with her, she'd throttle the weasel.

Twice.

At the station no-one answered. She shook her head. Stupid. Gerry didn't work Sundays – he had footy or cricket. And it seemed Karen was out on a call. Lisa headed back home, where she got her gloves then wrapped the bodies in a plastic bag. Outside, she paused at her garbage bin. Collection wasn't until next week and the forecast called for heat. Best to take the mice out of town a bit and leave them for birds or other scavengers.

She chucked them on the passenger floor and headed for Swallow's Road. Once the bush rose up around her she pulled into a gravel truck stop. An old, tan Land Cruiser was parked beside one of the picnic benches that no-one ever seemed to use.

It looked like the Healy's vehicle – a rear mudflap missing, just like Clint's car. She collected the mice and climbed from her Holden, approaching the Land Cruiser. The plastic bag swished as it swung from her grip. The cab was empty. Had it broken down? She circled the vehicle. The passenger door hung open, hidden from view from the highway. A picture of Clint Healy with his grandkids was taped to the dash.

So it was his car. Where was he?

"Clint?" Nothing. "Clint, are you all right?"

Lisa turned a slow circle. There. A hint of colour. A leg and a boot? She left the car, feet crunching on the gravel, a chill climbing her spine as she walked.

The bag of mice hit the ground.

Deep in the grass lay Clint Healy.

Unmoving. On his back, head turned away, flies buzzed over a wet slice in his stomach. More blood and the hint of intestine – black. One of his hands lay twisted up near his chest, tainted blue.

"God!"

She spun away, legs weak as she wobbled back toward the Cruiser. What was happening in Lidelson? Entrails everywhere! Like a nightmare... or a horror movie. She leaned against the tray and steadied her breathing.

Who would kill Clint? It didn't make sense; he was a nice guy.

She pulled her mobile, almost dropped it, fumbling to dial triple zero. Then she hung up and called the station. It'd be quicker if someone was actually –

"Lidelson Police Station, Karen speaking."

"Karen, it's Lisa Thomas. I've just found Clint Healy –

he's dead." She sounded too calm for someone who'd just found a body.

Something smacked down on the other end of the line. "What?"

"I'm on Swallow's Road at the first truck stop. Looks like he's been slashed."

"I'm on my way."

Lisa lowered her phone and stumbled back to the Holden, where she got in and sucked in a long breath, releasing it slowly. What was going on?

Death, death and more death.

Chapter 7.

The station had coffee.

Lisa used the mug to keep her hands still. Even in the hot station, the warmth was somehow welcome. Years of handling dead animals hadn't prepared her for finding a dead man, let alone one who had been cut open.

Karen sat across from her, a scuffed table between them as she fiddled with a recording device. "Piece of shit always does this." Her hair was caught in a tight bun and a speck of blood was visible beneath a silver stud in her ear.

"I can write my statement, if you like?" Lisa offered.

"It's fine. Good to have it on tape." Karen thumped the deck and a red light flicked on. "There." She placed it in the centre of the table and got the formalities of names and dates out of the way. "All right. Tell me what happened this morning."

"Ah, like I said at the truck stop. I was heading out of town to get rid of some dead mice. Someone had put them on my front step as a joke, I guess."

Karen nodded, her expression encouraging.

"I noticed a Land Cruiser at the truck stop on Swallow's Road."

"Did you recognise it?"

"I thought it was Clint Healy's so I went to see what he was up to. The Toyota was empty. I called his name but no-one answered."

"What did you do next?"

"I checked the cab and the passenger door was open. It was empty so I looked around." She tried to swallow but her mouth was too dry. "Clint lay in the grass and he wasn't moving. There was a gash in his stomach. He looked dead, he was dead."

"Did you touch him?"

"No. I called the station and waited in my car."

"All right, thank you, Miss Thomas." Karen clicked the tape off. "All done. How are you feeling?"

"A bit numb." Despite the promise of comfort from the coffee, she hadn't taken a sip yet. Clint had been a penny-pincher but other than that, a nice guy. A grandfather. Dad's age. "Who'd have wanted to kill him?"

"That's what we're going to find out," Karen said.

"Billy Brown?"

"Too easy – but we're certainly going to visit him anyway." Karen paused. "About those mice – you said there were entrails too?"

"That was another time." It almost sounded stupid, saying it aloud. "You think I'm in danger?"

Karen pursed her lips. "Better to be safe than sorry. Can anyone stay with you for a few days?"

Really? Was it that bad? "You're getting me a bit worried."

"Just want you to be safe is all. It's probably not related to the death."

"Think so?"

"I do," Karen said with a smile. "I reckon whatever happened up at that truck stop had nothing to do with any of us. Not you, not the Browns." She lifted an eyebrow. "You heard of ice?"

"The drug?"

"Right. People still seem to think it's a city drug but it's here too, I'm seeing more and more of it."

"And you think it's responsible?"

"Well, it screws with people pretty bad. Makes them violent, like, frothing at the mouth violent. Makes them more irrational too."

"You think it was random?"

"Sadly for Clint's family, I do. But we won't know for sure until after the autopsy."

Lisa shifted in her seat. "I guess I'll head home then?"

"Go for it. And call a friend or even stay at your dad's."

She nodded. "Maybe I will."

As she headed outside, Gerry pulled into the station. "Are you all right?" he asked as he stepped out of his car.

"You heard?"

"Everyone has."

"I'm okay."

He hesitated slightly, then gave her shoulder a gentle squeeze. "Atta girl. I better get in there, there's a big shot coming in from out of town." He paused. "And I just visited Ben. Told him to keep his distance. I let him know I'd be watching too."

"Thank you," Lisa said. "How'd he take it?"

"Didn't like it. But he'll do as he's told if he knows what's good for him."

"And the entrails? Because, I found some mice this morning."

"Shit." His brow was furrowed. "To be honest, I didn't think it was him. Maybe I'm wrong. I'll check on you later, if you like?"

"Yeah, thanks." It would be better to know for sure. If Ben was responsible, at least he was a jerk she knew. If it was some random creep...wasn't that worse?

Gerry headed inside and she leaned against her car door, keys in hand. Was it really a good thing that Gerry had been to see Ben? Felt like the right thing to do before, but now that she'd seen Ben a few times...it brought his pettiness and anger back. Two of Ben's favourites. What if the bastard used Gerry's visit as an excuse?

Calling Steph might not be a bad idea at all.

*

After she checked on Dad, who seemed occupied searching for an old book in the shed, she dragged herself home and put a movie on while she waited for Steph or Robert, even Matthew from the pub, to call back. Eventually she switched off the TV and returned to pacing. Who was trying to scare her? And did it have anything to do with Clint's death? An ice-addict could have been responsible for the killing – but no way was someone that trashed likely to go out and collect dead animals and place them on her doorstep.

She paused in the hall, standing before the small painting

of a tree on a hilltop. Another one of Dad's – one of the last ones he painted before he stopped. It was a nightscape, pale moonlight filtering the scene. A branch was broken but the rest of the tree stood tall.

Her hand closed into a fist.

Whoever was messing with her would find that it took a lot more to really spook her.

Night fell and she ate a dinner of pasta on the couch while the TV rambled. She checked her phone – constantly. Stupid, just sitting around and waiting. She got up and put the washing on, snapping the machine's lid down. Inspired by Dad's tree, she rummaged around in the spare room for hammer and hook before hanging the Monet print she'd been holding onto for ages. *San Giorgio Maggiore at Twilight* – its bright orange, almost like fire, caught the eye against the plain wall.

Before the washing cycle ended lights flashed across the front windows and wheels crunched in her drive. The engine cut and a bottle smashed. "Lisa!"

A slurred voice.

"Lisa, get out here, you bitch."

Ben.

She snatched the hammer from the kitchen bench and strode to the front door. If he was pissed he'd probably break the door down. She hit the switch for the outside light before leaving the house, stopping on the front step.

Ben paused mid-stumble, can in hand. Heavy beer, no doubt. "Go away, Ben," she told him. He cast an unsteady shadow in the front light; it stretched back to his Commodore.

"What's wrong with you?"

She crossed her arms, hammer gripped tight. "Go home;

you're drunk."

He squinted at her then laughed. "What are you going to do with that?"

"You'll find out if you don't piss off."

"Yeah? Going to do it yourself this time, are you?" He plucked at his shirt; the neck was ripped. "No? Well, I don't see your boyfriend anywhere."

"What are you talking about?"

"That fucking pig," he spat.

"Ben, get out of here."

He lurched forward. "No. This is bullshit. I come back, I drive all the way back from fucking Queensland and try and apologise and you sic your pet cop on me?"

She raised the hammer and he stopped.

"Fine." He hurled his can into the yard and turned to his car, muttering as he went. He got in and after some fumbling and swearing, jerked out of the drive, smashing into a letterbox then screeching along the street. Burnt rubber filled the air.

Lisa stood on the step, hammer in hand, until the sound of his engine faded to black.

Chapter 8.

Lisa was on the phone with Steph the next morning when a knock rang through the house. Gerry was waiting on the doorstep, holding his hat, and she waved him in as she finished up the call.

"I'm sorry, we had a plumbing emergency," Steph said. "Typical Monday morning." The clatter of cutlery and dishes filled the background. "So, are you doing okay?"

"Yeah, I'm fine." Lisa paused. Clint's face had been so, so pale. Nothing like the way the man really looked. "I thought the job might prepare me for death a bit, you know? But a human body... it's not the same." She glanced at Gerry, but he was studying the paintings on the wall. "Are you guys okay?"

"Oh, honey. We're fine. Want me to come over on my lunch break?"

"How about I make you dinner instead? You've been so good to me lately."

"Deal. You just pick a time," she said.

"How about next week? Maybe Friday?"

"Great, I'll talk to you soon."

Gerry turned to her. His expression was apologetic. "I heard. I'm sorry, Lisa."

"It's not your fault."

"No, it is; I leaned on him pretty hard."

"Don't worry. And Mrs Anderson was fine about the letterbox. Told her I'd pay for it," she said, heading to the kitchen. "Did you want a drink?"

He shook his head. "Look, I can back off a bit if you like. I'll still watch him, though. I know what he's like."

"Maybe." She tried to smile. She didn't really want that, but if the visits kept provoking Ben, then maybe.

"All right." He rolled his sleeves over his forearms and leaned against the counter. "Actually, I did want to ask you something about Clint."

That pale, dead face flashed before her eyes again, and her hand tightened on her cup. "Okay."

"I checked at the morgue and there's some evidence that it was an animal attack."

"What?" Lisa put her cup down with a frown.

"That's why I wanted to see you. That gash had rough edges."

"Claws?"

"And we don't have bears here."

"You think a kangaroo did this?"

"Maybe."

"I don't know, Gerry. There's a record of someone dying from a kangaroo attack up in New South Wales. A hunter back in the '30s, I think it was. It's pretty rare though."

"Well, I can only tell you what I've been told," he said. "If it's true, the doc thinks it was a big one. Really big."

Big like Pumps' Great White Roo? That was even less likely. "It still doesn't make much sense."

"Want to take a look at the site, anyway? I'm not sold on it myself, but I want to rule it out. We're certain the wound didn't come from a blade."

"I've got a couple of jobs today but I'll push them back if you like?"

"Thanks, Lisa. It's probably a waste of time, so I appreciate it."

"Can't hurt to look." She smiled this time then made the calls before joining him in the police car. A St Kilda Football Club air-freshener hung from his rear-view mirror, swaying with the turns as he drove out of town, eyes on the road. "So, any more animal parts on your doorstep?"

Trees flashed by in green streaks. "Not yet."

He glanced at her before returning his attention to the road. "Expecting more?"

"It wouldn't surprise me."

"Thought about a camera?"

"Yeah?"

"It can be expensive, but you can get motion-activated ones. Wireless. Saves battery and space on your computer. That way you'll know if it's Ben."

"Maybe I should." But the idea of letting Ben drive her to all that...maybe not.

He pulled into the truck stop. "Think about it." His gaze met hers. "I could...I could let you use our discount."

Had he been going to say something else? But he didn't elaborate. "Thanks, Gerry. I'll definitely think about it," she said and hopped out, following him to the weathered bench.

The Land Cruiser was gone and in its place, white and blue police tape criss-crossed the area. He lifted one section and she ducked beneath, moving to the grass where she'd found Clint. Not all the blades had sprung back up just yet.

She stepped into the trees and searched the ground; no sign of tracks. No droppings, no torn earth. No fur left behind. If a roo had attacked Clint, there would have been evidence of it somewhere. Maybe even signs of grazing or droppings, but nothing suggested that.

Gerry kept a few paces behind. She widened her search but still nothing.

She rose from where she'd crouched by a half-sunken rock slab. "Maybe the killer used something that wasn't steel."

"No sign of roos?"

"None. They would have torn up the earth a bit when they took off," she said, rising and dusting her hands against one another.

He sighed. "All right, let's take you back then."

"Disappointed?" she asked as their feet crunched over the leaves.

"An ice addict means two lives ruined, you know?"

"You think that's what happened."

"Still too early to tell." He held branches out of her way. "But someone that out of it could have used anything. Didn't have to be a knife."

It was harder to keep Clint's face out of her mind. They drove back in silence, a comfortable silence, and Lisa thanked him at the front door before heading inside and collecting her cleaning gear. Then it was into the Holden and off to the first job.

By midday, she'd pulled into the bakery.

Ronnie was roaring with laughter when she opened the door, bell chiming with her entry. His customers smiled along but the snub-nosed fellow before the register, clutching a brown paper bag, was red-faced.

Billy Brown. "Bullshit," the young man said.

"No, Billy, you're talking rot. The police don't have it in for you, they think it was someone on drugs," said Ronnie.

"So why they been around twice already?"

"Look son, your pies are getting cold."

Billy shook his head.

Someone lowered their voice. "Who's keeping an eye on your sheep, then, Billy?"

"What?" He whirled on the other customers but no-one spoke and he eyed them each before storming out. Lisa gave him room and approached the counter to put in her order over snickering, some of which came from the high school kids. Too bad it was the holidays – they were always underfoot this time of year. But that wasn't fair – was it that long ago that she'd been bored enough to visit the street just to see her friends and do nothing? Maybe not.

"Ronnie, can I have a steak, bacon and pepper pie?" she asked.

He snapped his fingers. "Sure thing."

She selected a coke from the fridge while he readied her lunch, then handed over a ten. "Thanks, Ronnie."

"Before you go, I've heard something that might interest you," he said.

"Yeah?"

"Heard about your strange problems."

"With the kangaroos?"

"Yeah – and the blood and guts part."

A little shiver crept along her shoulders. Was everyone listening now? "Have you heard who did it?"

He drummed his fingers on the glass counter. "Nope, but I ran into Phil this morning and he said he saw someone carrying a bag down your street the other day when he was on one of his midnight jogs, the fool. He'll get hit by a car one of these days."

"Really? Is he still at work?"

"Should be."

"Thanks, Ronnie. I'll go see him."

She took a seat in the bakery, pressed up against the window like a display in a museum, ate her lunch then headed for the general store.

Phil was out back when she rang the plump little bell beside the register. He was wiping his hands with a purple-stained towel when he exited the storeroom. "Lisa, good to see you."

"Hi, Phil. Having a bit of trouble back there?"

"Dropped my cranberry juice." He shook his head. "I was enjoying it too."

"Always the way." She grinned. "I just spoke to Ronnie and he said you saw something in my street?"

"I did." He tossed the towel into a bin and rubbed at his stained hands as he spoke. "I was out jogging. It didn't really register until after Stacey at the post office told me about your problem. I thought it was pretty damn strange."

Good to know the small town gossip train was working at its usual peak levels. "Think it could have been my ex?"

"Shorter than Ben, I think. And he was a bit far away, just dressed in black and carrying a pretty big bag. That's why I noticed him."

"Well, I guess that's good." Though if it wasn't Ben himself, it didn't mean Ben didn't put someone up to it. If he was even involved. The alternative was still worse. Someone random. Someone she didn't know. Some freak. If that was it...shit, why?

"Doesn't look like you think it's that good."

She offered a small smile. "At least if it's not Ben it means he's not crazy." Just drunk. And violent. "Well, thanks Phil, I better get back to work."

"Sure thing."

By the time she finished her cleaning jobs – covering Pete Ascot's fox again – it was dark and she rushed home to leap into a hot shower. Afterwards, she paced the kitchen while a pot of pasta bubbled away. Gerry was right about the camera. Or at least, about trying something to find out what was going on. Maybe it was worth getting something, maybe not as elaborate as he had in mind, but it wouldn't hurt to see what her options were.

But tomorrow – now she was going to get some sleep. And to hell with whoever it was leaving things on her step.

She climbed beneath soft blankets but left the hallway light on.

Chapter 9.

Nothing tainted her front step the next morning but the backyard was a different story.

Another dead body.

This time a koala, its grey form slumped against the clothesline. Its dark nose still bore traces of moisture.

She sunk to her knees beside it, stroking the fur. "What happened to you?"

No answer, just like the others. Poor guy. And even though there were no obvious wounds, it was not an accident. No fires in the hills to drive him out, no eucalypt in the garden. A nature reserve ran behind Chambers Street but it was hardly bushland. Lisa climbed onto the back fence.

An elderly couple walked the trail, arm in arm. The woman blinked at her. Lisa smiled. "Hi."

"Hello dear." They moved on.

Lisa scanned the reserve. Nothing stood out. Everything was as it should be. Green grass just turning yellow, a few Banksia bushes and a winding walking path of pale gravel.

A mystery, just like the mythical white roo. She shook her head and started to climb down.

Wait.

A hole rested at the base of her fence. She hauled herself over, thumping onto the grass. The hole was empty, deep, exposing the buried wire. Bigger than anything a rabbit would dig. Whoever made it had obviously given up. From the rear, the fence was too high so she walked around.

Gerry was knocking on her front door again.

"Gerry?"

His face was grim when he turned. "Lisa, your dad's in hospital. He had a fall."

She froze. Dad had fallen? "Where? Is he all right? Which hospital?"

"He hit his head." Gerry led her to his car. "Come on, I'll take you to him."

Lisa jumped into the cruiser. "What happened?" She laced and unlaced her fingers in her lap. Just like Mum used to. Gerry backed out of the driveway, put his foot down and the engine roared. He flicked the siren on and cut through the traffic, explaining that her father had fallen down the steps at the post office. Lisa barely heard the rest. It didn't make sense. Dad was usually pretty good on his feet, how had this happened?

"You know, it might be for the best," he was saying.

"Huh?"

Gerry slipped around a log truck, using the only overtaking lane on the winding road. They were heading out of town, toward Yarsdale, the only hospital in the area. "Have you thought about seeing if he'll go into a home?"

She did. Sometimes. But weren't there other options?

There had to be. "I don't know."

"It's probably the right thing."

"It's a rotten thing, Gerry."

He winced at her words, but continued. "But you can't care for him, can you? If he's getting worse. You can see that, right?"

"Yes. But I don't want to do it. To reduce him like that." She shook her head. "Just collapse him down to a single room and a handful of possessions. I don't want to take him from his home and transform him into a...a patient. If he goes there that's it – God's waiting room. He's only just turned seventy, damn it." Lisa slapped the passenger arm.

He was silent a moment. "I'm sorry."

"No-one called me."

"Well, I saw it happen and I got him into the ambulance." He glanced at her. "I wanted to tell you myself."

She sighed. It wasn't his fault. "No, I'm sorry." She was lucky he'd been around. He was pretty great like that. Back when she finally reported Ben, when she finally left him, Gerry had been the one to chase Ben out of town. And especially since Dad got sick, Gerry had found a way to check on her regularly.

Lisa squeezed his arm where it rested on the shift. "And thanks."

He nodded.

They drove on with just the growl of the engine and the shriek of sirens until Yarsdale appeared, its old-fashioned buildings and big verandahs flashing by until the hospital appeared, a white blur through the tears that had sprung up. He had to be all right. Had to be. Come on, Dad.

Gerry had them in the right ward quick smart, then he

disappeared to find coffee and a nurse was suddenly taking Lisa to Dad's bed, pulling back the curtain...

Her heart flipped.

When did he get so small?

All the white sheets and pillows propping him up, as though they were keeping him alive. She half-ran, half-stumbled around the bed to stroke his white hair. "Dad."

The frown line in her father's brow had eased as he slept, one side of his head covered in bandages. A tiny cut on his jaw, where he'd probably nicked himself shaving that morning, stood in stark contrast to the paleness of his skin.

The nurse opened the window a crack and left.

Lisa looked around. Gerry was still hunting for coffee it seemed, but that was fine. Time alone couldn't hurt. And the beep of the ECG could keep her company. She leant back in the hard chair beside the hospital bed as the curtain slid open.

"Lisa Thomas?" A doctor in a white coat held a chart, her face brimming with weariness. "I'm Doctor Bagnato."

She stood. "Will he be all right?"

"He's recovering but we won't know what sort of damage has been done until he wakes."

"Later tonight?"

"Most likely. But once we know, we can make sure there's nothing serious going on. He's likely to make a good recovery, he seems tough."

"So he's not stable yet?"

"He is but head wounds can be unpredictable." Her voice grew a little firmer. "I can't make promises, I hope you understand."

Lisa looked to her father. "I do."

"The ambulance report says he fell down some steps?"

"I wasn't there, but he's usually more steady on his feet. I think...he might have Alzheimer's or something."

The doctor tilted her head. "What makes you say that?"

"He's having more memory problems than in the past and sometimes he just seems lost in space, staring."

"Have you been to see his GP?"

Lisa shook her head. "Not yet."

"You should make an appointment."

"I will." No more excuses now.

A hand came to rest on her shoulder. "This is the best place for him for now."

"I know."

"There's some paperwork at the nurse's station when you're ready."

Lisa nodded but didn't move for a long time.

*

It was dark when Gerry dropped her off with a promise to check on her tomorrow and she dragged herself inside with a huge sigh. Even though Dad hadn't woken, he seemed more stable at least, and coming home drained the tension from her body.

She hit the kitchen light and a small smile graced her lips. Even her old toaster – just sitting there on the bench – even that silly silver rectangle was a welcome sight.

"Hello, Lisa."

She jumped.

Ben moved into the kitchen from the darkened lounge. His eyes were flat and he moved with purpose. Not drunk this time, just angry.

"What are you doing in here?" She took a step back.

"I'm just leaving, actually." He started around the bench and she edged toward the kitchen drawer. Where the bigger knives lay. Her pulse had already doubled.

"Get out, Ben."

He paused in the hall. "I've written a letter, since you won't let me talk."

Then he was gone.

She tore a knife from the drawer and locked the front door, then did the same for each window and the back and sliding door too. No evidence of how he got in, nothing broken and nothing open. Bastard, bastard, bastard.

The letter sat on her pillow.

She dropped the knife.

"You prick." Lisa snatched the letter and strode to the kitchen, where she grabbed matches from beside the stove, striking one and snapping the head. She struck another. It lit and she held the tiny flame beneath the envelope. The edges curled orange and black and once the flame grew, she dropped it into the sink and let it burn down to ashes.

Too far. Too much today; not with Dad hurt. Ben had gone too fucking far. He'd done it just to show her that he could break in anytime he liked. Back to the old bullshit. Control, control, control. Well, not again.

She had her mobile out in a flash, dialling Lidelson Station.

It kept ringing. What time was it? Was Karen out on a call? Maybe – but it wasn't a twenty-four hour station either. When her call was automatically transferred to Yarsdale Station, she hung up half-way through the officer's answer.

They were half an hour away.

Instead, she yanked open the bottom drawer and grabbed her hammer and then her keys before storming to the car. She roared out of Chambers Street and into the centre of town, bursting through the yellow light before it flashed red then skidding onto the boulevard that swept around the park. Nice houses, big yards and a quiet street.

And right where Steph said it was – Ben's new place.

Two storeys and a nice cream-coloured fence with matching trim on the windows.

Just the kind of house they used to dream about.

"Bastard."

The windows were dark and the 'For Sale' sign had been obscured by a big slab of a 'Sold' sticker. Good for him. How wonderful. She pulled into the driveway and got out without cutting the engine, striding over the unfinished landscaping to the front window. "Prick." She swung the hammer with a shout, its head crashing through the glass.

Next window.

More glass shattered.

And the next one, until she'd done the whole front of the house. It didn't take long but lights still came on in neighbouring properties.

"There, you bastard." A message of her own.

Lisa leapt back into the car and tore away, security lights fading in her rear mirror.

Chapter 10.

Lisa lifted the corner of the bed, tucked the pale blue sheet in and stood, wiping sweat from her forehead. She'd opened the window but there was no breeze, just laughter and the clink of cutlery on breakfast plates from the pub's rear garden. Another freaking hot day – but then, that was summer. No real choice in the matter. Hot day and night with only the ugly chill of air-conditioning to break it up.

At least the sunsets were long.

"She's down here, I think." Bruce's voice drifted up the passage. Two pairs of footsteps.

She straightened, sliding the bucket of cleaning gear aside. If Bruce was stupid enough to bring Ben along...

Bruce shuffled into the room, accidently knocking a dresser with his shoe as he let Gerry in. Gerry wore jeans and a faded Cold Chisel shirt, his dark hair was a little messy – must've been a day off.

He gave her a fleeting smile. "I guess you know why I'm here."

She nodded, taking a seat on the bed.

Bruce rubbed the back of his neck. "Ah, well, yeah. I'll get back to it I reckon."

"Thanks, Bruce." Gerry leant against the doorframe. "I just wanted to warn you that you were seen on Overlook Boulevard and Ben has already been to the station to make a report. He told Karen he knows it was you."

"He mention what he did?"

"No."

"Broke in to my place and waited for me to get home last night. Even wrote a letter, which he left on my bed."

Gerry frowned, fury flashing in his eyes – there and gone. "You shouldn't have to put up with this, Lisa. You can have him charged. Do you still have the letter?"

"I burnt it."

"We could have used it to help show he broke in."

Lisa swore under her breath. Stupid.

"What did it say?"

"I didn't read it." She stood. "I'm not interested in anything he has to say. And you know he's not going to be scared by an intervention order."

He started to speak but stopped. "Fair enough. How's your dad?"

"Still at the hospital. I got a call earlier, he's going to be okay. I'm going out again today, I just have to catch up on a few jobs first."

"Good. Well, I thought you'd like to know that Karen and I won't be pursuing the matter – right away at least. I plan to drag my feet a bit on this one." He paused. "Hope it felt good."

"Last night it felt amazing. Now I feel like an idiot."

He chuckled. "Well, don't beat yourself up. Worry about your dad for now."

"Thanks, Gerry. I owe you, you know."

His smile widened. "Buy me coffee one day."

"Deal."

She watched him head back up the passage. He was a good guy – he didn't come on too strong. And maybe he had more than coffee in mind, maybe he didn't. Steph seemed to think he did. Yet Gerry had never pushed for anything. Either way...Lisa smiled to herself as she resumed tidying. Once she finished, she could finally head back onto the road and get out to Yarsdale to see Dad.

Her phone rang, a cry muffled by her jeans pocket. It might be the hospital. She tore the mobile out.

Pumps.

What did he want? She hit 'answer'. "Mr Johnson?"

"Lisa, is that you?" He was out of breath.

"Yes. Are you all right?"

"It's the roo – I've seen her again."

She bit back a sigh. "Yeah?"

"Something's not right though; she's gone wild."

"What do you mean?"

A shout came through the phone and then a clattering sound. More muffled noises and then the line went dead.

Lisa frowned at the phone; that didn't sound good. The farm was on the way to the hospital...Or she could send Gerry around. She grabbed her bag, heading down the corridor. No. She'd given him enough trouble lately and he'd obviously taken the day off. Knowing Pumps it wouldn't be too serious, surely...maybe just drive out quickly and see for herself, before she bothered Gerry again.

Bruce handed her an envelope from the bar and she thanked him as she rushed out the door. "Gotta run, Bruce."

If she was quick, she could check on Pumps and Dad, then get back in time for her shift with Robert. He wouldn't mind if she was late but still...

The road was quiet as usual and when she turned into Anne's Lane she was tapping the wheel with her thumb. What if something had happened? Pumps' old, mustard-coloured Datsun crouched in the driveway. No smoke rose from the chimney and the ever-present kitchen light was dark.

But the door stood wide open.

Lisa hopped from the car. "Mr Johnson?"

Silence.

Inside, the kitchen revealed a half-eaten breakfast – two big bites out of toast and jam, tea untouched. "Hello? Mr Johnson?" Nothing. The rest of the rooms were empty – bed unmade and radio muttering away in the lounge, fireplace cold. "It's Lisa Thomas, are you all right?"

Her feet creaked on the floorboards.

"God damn it, Pumps – where are you?"

Back outside, she leant on the gate and scanned the property; paddocks stretched in green folds. The shed. She ran over, heat from the sun bouncing off tin. The dents remained, tufts of hay peeking through. The door was closed but unchained. She dragged it open and stepped into a dim interior.

Hay bales towered over a large shape spread across the earthen floor.

She blinked.

A white kangaroo.

Its tail curved beneath long legs and the head lay tucked into its body but there it was. Had the roo stood, its bulk would have been three metres – maybe four from toe to head. Was it dead?

She crept closer, narrowing her eyes.

The fur was very clean. And regular. No uneven patches, just pure white. And the head appeared a little...deflated around the neck. She nudged it with her foot. The mouth was empty of teeth and both eyes had a glass-look.

Lisa bent and lifted the head, which sagged over her hand. "Holy shit."

A fake. What the hell was Pumps playing at?

She stormed from the shed and spun on her heel. "Mr Johnson, where are you? Hello?" She shouted the last word. Only a faint echo of her own voice from across the fields. Cows chewed at the grass, utterly disinterested. She grabbed her mobile and dialled, pacing before the shed.

Still no answer. She looked up from the phone and flinched.

Pumps lay slumped across the tractor seat.

"Mr Johnson!" She ran to the giant wheel and climbed up, shaking his shoulder. The skin was still warm beneath his flannelette. "Are you all right?"

Pumps rolled aside, limbs almost liquid in their looseness. His face was pale and twisted in a grimace but he did not respond. No marks on his body. Heart attack? A .308 lay across his knees, scope catching the sun. "Shit." She held her finger against his throat, moving it around. Where the hell was his pulse?

"Come on." No response, no trickle of life sliding beneath his skin.

Lisa stepped back and swallowed, hard. Everywhere she turned, another dead body. She lifted her phone, dialling the police. Should have called Gerry after all.

Chapter 11.

"It's not your fault, darl," Dad said. A warmer tinge to his cheeks made him appear better but he still wasn't the same. He sat up in bed, noon sunlight from open curtains near-blinding on the white walls caused him to squint each time he leant for his cup of water. Just how much he understood as to how he'd ended up in the hospital wasn't clear.

She didn't mention all the dead bodies she'd been finding over the last few days – and she still had to talk to that detective up from the city. Gerry had let her leave Pumps' farm after only a few questions so she could make visiting hours. Thankfully, because if she found one more dead body... But that wasn't fair to Clint or Pumps. What had happened to them? And Pumps...was it really his heart?

What was the rifle for?

"Dad, I feel responsible. I should have helped you more."

He narrowed his eyes a little. "Don't be silly. You've got a life to live."

"So do you."

He waved away her words.

Maybe now was the time. She opened her mouth, to ask about making an appointment for a home, but let it close. How could she even suggest it? "I could move in with you." She blurted it out.

Now he smiled. "That really what you were going to say?"

"No. But I mean it."

He looked away. "I've thought about it, you know. I'm having a lot of trouble remembering things. Even rang a place and spoke to one of the ladies there. She seemed nice enough. They've got rooms that overlook the river."

"Dad."

His lips were pressed into a tight line. "It's not getting better, sweetie."

She took his hand. "There's medication we can try, isn't there? We'll go see Dr Albert; he can prescribe something."

"Maybe."

"Well, we should try them first, anyway."

"They aren't cheap, I'm going to bet."

"It's fine. We'll find a way."

He nodded, blinking hard as he squeezed her hand.

A nurse bustled in with a tray of food – the best thing on it looked to be the crimson-coloured jelly. "How are you feeling today, Mr Thomas?"

"Not too bad." He squinted at her nametag. "Nurse Peterson."

"You can call me Mel, you know." She arranged the tray and smiled at Lisa. "He's doing quite well."

"That's good. So, do you think he'll be able to go home?"

"I don't know but I'll make sure Doctor Bagnato calls you." Mel glanced at the clock. "I'll have to boot you out in a few minutes."

"I understand, thank you."

"Eat it all, Mr Thomas," Mel said from the door.

He grinned. "I'll try but it isn't exactly steak and crème brûlée, you've got here."

"In a public hospital? Good luck." She chuckled as she left.

"I'd better go too." Lisa stood. "I'll be back tomorrow, hopefully to take you home."

"Got my fingers crossed."

She slipped into the hall and sucked in a huge breath before heading down the white corridor.

*

Headlights cut into the darkness and Lisa slouched in the passenger seat, the hum of the ute barely audible over the slurping of Robert's juice. She glanced at him. "Inhaling that one, are you?"

He lowered the bottle with a snort. "It keeps me alert. And the straw's too thin."

"Yeah, yeah."

"Just concentrate on your side of the road."

"I am." She focused on the gravel beside the highway, pale in the headlights. Hopefully the roo wasn't hurt too badly. A spinal or hind-leg injury and it was probably too late. They'd have to put the kangaroo down. Every call brought the same tension – Robert would have to be the one to get the .22 from the toolbox.

Handling a gun was still...difficult. Not because she couldn't – Granddad taught her – but not since the time they hit a deer in his old truck, coming home late one night after a netball match in Yarsdale. He'd told her to stay in the cab but she had to see.

The deer lay broken, bleeding on the side of the road, eyes vacant – steam rising from blood in the night air.

"Running blind," he said, his blue eyes hard.

"Why? Couldn't she hear the car?"

He pointed to a small hole in the deer's side. "Someone's been out shooting."

After that night, no more practice with paper targets on the giant oak; she hadn't fired a gun since.

"So how's your dad?" Robert switched the radio on but turned it down.

"He's okay – I'm hoping to bring him home tomorrow."

"What'll you do? Is it dementia?"

"I don't know yet. But I made an appointment with Dr Albert. We'll see what it is and then maybe see if medication helps, I guess."

Robert slowed. A van appeared in the lights – a figure leaning against it. Painted purple, it had mag wheels and surf stickers on the back. "Great, it's a couple of kids," she said.

"Maybe not – how many kids would stick around after hitting a roo, let alone call it in?"

"Some would, but I think you're right."

Robert parked the ute behind the van then cut the engine. "Let's see how bad it is."

She followed him out into the blast of headlights. On the shoulder beside the bitumen lay a young roo, a big grey. A clean hole at the shoulder bled onto the gravel. It looked more like a bullet hole rather than an accident.

"What's going on?" Robert bent by the kangaroo then glanced up at the guy leaning against the van. "He's not alive. And you didn't hit him."

The driver shrugged as he looked away. Was he familiar? Lanky, sullen face – it looked like Steve – Ben's friend. "Steve?"

Robert turned from the kangaroo. "You know this guy?"

"He's one of Ben's friends."

"You think wasting our time is funny?" Robert glared at Steve.

Steve snorted. "Just shut-up, mate."

Robert shot to his feet but a figure leapt from the trees, swinging something at his legs. The blow toppled him and Steve pounced. His fist thumped into Robert's face when he tried to rise. Steve and the other shape hauled Robert to his feet. "You weren't supposed to be here."

The other one was Fathead. He held a bat in one hand and his broad face was pale but he didn't release the groaning Robert.

"What the hell are you two doing?" she shouted.

Hands gripped her shoulders. The warm stench of beer on a man's breath brushed her neck. A familiar scent – for all the wrong reasons. She thrashed her way free and spun.

Ben stood before her, his face twisted in rage. The pink scar stood out on his cheek. He pointed a shaking finger at her. "Where's your cop buddy now, huh?"

"You piece of shit," she spat. "Stop it. Now!"

He stepped close, clawing at her arm. She fought and he swung an open hand. Her vision blacked out momentarily and a ringing in her ears followed. She stumbled, but Ben pulled her close, shaking her.

Robert was shouting and Ben snarled across the headlights. "Shut him up."

A thump and Steve sniggered.

Ben's thumbs bit into her arms. "What are you doing, smashing my windows then telling the pigs to ignore me? Well? What's that about, Lisa?" He shook her again. "Did you even read the letter?"

Lisa slammed her heel onto his foot.

He fell back with a shout. She charged Steve, swinging at him. He ducked away and Robert fell to the ground. Hands gripped her again, flinging her against the ute. She bounced off the hood and thumped onto the gravel with a grunt.

The same hands hauled her up and then a rock cracked into her head – or so it seemed. Purple vans, headlights, trees and roads spun, but she didn't fall.

"Ben, stop!"

Lisa frowned. Was that Fathead?

"You keep out of this, James – you hear me? You've done your job."

"She's hurt. Let's just get out of here."

Another voice. Steve maybe. "You said she'd be alone, Ben."

"Well, she isn't, is she? Get the others." He dragged her over to the kangaroo – shoving her to her knees.

She coughed, spitting blood. It hit the stones with a splat. "What do you want?"

Ben said nothing but Steve soon appeared with something in his arms. He dumped the shape – a wallaby, it's head lolling to the side as it settled. A fox was next, then another wallaby and even a black snake. All limp and lifeless, blood glistening in the headlights.

"You're sick," she cried.

Ben grunted. "You tell anyone about this and I'll make sure a lot more of your friends get shot, understand? This'll look like a friggen picnic."

"This is how you want to win me back?"

"Bitch." He shoved her aside and crunched back to the van, snarling at his friends to follow. Wheels spun on gravel as they backed onto the road, tearing off into the night. The sound of bottles shattering followed and the heavy smell of exhaust filled the roadside.

Lisa dragged herself across to Robert, who lay on his back, breathing hard. "I'm fine," he said. "Are you okay?"

"Yeah," she gasped out. Her lip stung in the night air, as did a graze on her head. She winced when she touched it and her fingertips came back wet. What the fuck was happening? Ben wasn't just drunk – he was insane. Worse than before; now he was involving others.

"What was that about?" Robert asked, dragging himself into a sitting position.

"I provoked him." She clasped her hands together to stop them shaking. "And he's drunk. I don't know."

"He's a sick bastard, that's what he is."

"I know." And he'd do just what he claimed too. If she went to Gerry, he'd be killing animals everywhere – it was obvious now, he was the one dumping the animals at her place. Just to get at her, just to keep her quiet. Prick. It was exactly like before. The threats. Holding violence over her. All of it. Years ago there was always the unspoken threat – that of expectation. She knew what he'd do if she angered him, he'd shown her enough times. Like the backhand into the bedroom wall when she threatened to tell someone what he'd done.

Lisa climbed to her feet, wiping at the side of her mouth. More blood. She'd have a fat lip tomorrow. "Here." She helped Robert up, who groaned. His eye was already swelling.

"Let me drive," he said at the car. "You might have a concussion."

She nodded as she climbed in. Robert fumbled with the keys a moment and she caught his arm. "Wait. The bodies. I don't want to leave them."

He groaned but opened the door.

Once they'd secured the bodies Robert left her to sprinkle what little salt she had thin across them. She stayed back a moment, trying to slow her breathing. God, they'd even killed a snake. What the hell could she do? Ben wasn't going to back down. She couldn't stop him even if she went to the police.

"I'm sorry," she said to the bodies, then returned to the ute.

Robert started back toward town, soon muttering to himself.

"What is it?"

"Bet the bastard has a licence. You know, for shooting. For culling, like other farmer families."

"You think I should tell Gerry."

"Shit yes. You can't let that bastard and his stupid friends get away with this. If you don't report it, I will. Someone has to stop him before he does it again. Who knows, maybe he even killed Clint and Pumps."

"What?" She spun her head to him, pain flaring in her neck. "Why would he do that?"

"Who knows? He's insane." Robert threw up a hand. "He

doesn't need a reason."

"Clint wasn't shot and Pumps had a heart attack," she said, trying to massage her neck.

"So? Let's just go to the police."

"I can't. He'll start shooting kangaroos and who knows what else if we do that. I know he will."

Robert shook his head.

"Please, Robert. At least until I think of something else."

"Like what? You're playing his game if you don't. Letting him control you again."

She lowered her voice. "You weren't there, Robert."

"I've heard enough."

"Pull over," she snapped.

He slowed the ute and pulled onto the shoulder where he wrenched the handbrake on. Headlights hit the pale trunks of gum trees. He looked to the darkness as he spoke, "What's your suggestion then?"

Something bubbly played on the radio. She flicked it off. What kind of idiot DJ played something that happy at ten pm? "I haven't got one. I just don't want him to kill any more roos."

He turned back. "Me either – so let's get him locked up."

"He'll make bail. Or he'll ask Steve or Fathead to do it."

Robert thumped the dash. "Well, I don't want him to get away with this. Any of them."

"I know."

He sighed. In the reflected light from the dash she could just make out his jaw working. "I don't know if I can let this go."

Lisa gave a slow nod; Robert was right. She *would* be letting Ben win if she gave in. Worse, she'd be falling back into the same old pattern of doing what she was told. Or being too afraid to do what was right. And that wasn't an option anymore. And truly, what could she do by herself? Against three of them. And one of them Ben. Ben with a gun.

They needed help.

"Let's go find Gerry then."

Chapter 12.

At first, Gerry stood silhouetted in the doorway dressed only in shorts and singlet, regarding them with a confused expression – but his mouth dropped open when he saw them properly. He pulled them inside. "What happened to you two?" His expression darkened. "Ben?"

"Who else?" Lisa said.

He led her to a kitchen table cluttered with newspapers, pulling a chair for her then Robert and waving for them to sit. He gathered up a manila folder of files and photographs, closing and placing it on the bench. "I'll make you some coffee."

She nodded, Robert joining her.

"What did he do?" He flicked the kettle. Mugs clinked as he pulled them from a wooden cupboard.

Lisa explained the trick phone call and the beating, including Steve and Fathead. "They'd shot all these animals and Ben told us he'd kill more if we went to the police and made it official. That's why I wanted to see you here."

Gerry raised an eyebrow. "So this isn't an official report?"

"It should be," Robert said, but he didn't push the issue.

"I don't know what to do," Lisa said. "He's worse than I've ever seen him."

"Worse than when he smashed up the pub the day I booted him out of town?" Gerry asked. He finished with the drinks and spread them across the table. They looked small in his big hands. One had a little grey Totoro figure on the side. "My niece's," he said when he noticed her gaze.

She nodded. "Yeah, worse than the pub."

"Well, you can get him and the others on assault, and a few more things. Ben would probably do jail time. With his history, it'd be easy."

"And in the meantime he'll be out while he waits for a court date and have months to run around killing things," she said.

"Or worse – he comes after you," Robert added.

Gerry put his mug down. "If you think he'd attack you again I need to know."

"No, he's not there yet."

Robert shook his head and Gerry raised an eyebrow. "Looks like he's hit you already. Both of you."

"I know him." Lisa said. "And you said it yourself, he's trying to control me not kill me. He'll probably try and blackmail me further, with the animals."

"This is pretty sick even for him," Gerry said. "He can't be stupid enough to think he can re-start your relationship like this."

"He's not thinking," Lisa said.

"So what are you going to do about it?" Robert asked. He was calmer now, but he sat straight on the chair.

"I don't know."

"Document everything," Gerry suggested. "You don't have to press charges tomorrow but the sooner the better. Take it seriously. You know I'll help you."

"Hmmm." Lisa frowned, hands wrapped around the warm mug. "I need something quicker than charges."

"Break his legs," Robert muttered.

Gerry took another sip. "I didn't hear that."

Lisa stood. "Let me sleep on it." She raised fingertips to her cheek and bottom lip, wincing.

Gerry held up a hand. "Wait, let me take some photos. I want to document this." Using his phone, he snapped a few shots of their injuries then walked them to the door.

"I'll drop you off then," Robert told Lisa. "Thanks for the drink, Gerry."

"No problems." Gerry said. "You should make it official, Lisa. I can't force you, but think about it."

"I will."

"Good. And I thought you'd like to know about Pumps Johnson," he added. "Pretty sure it was a heart attack, just waiting on confirmation. No idea why. Maybe it was just his time."

"But why call me?"

"Part of the white roo hoax?"

"He sounded afraid – and there was the gun. I dunno if he was acting."

"Well, the rifle's a dead end. No forensic evidence to say anyone else had touched it so it's part of his estate now."

"I didn't know he had much family left."

"There's a cousin interstate somewhere." He shook his head. "First Clint and Pumps and now you two. It's been a shitty week."

"It has."

"I'll see if I can find Ben – and don't argue with me, all right?" He took her by the shoulders, his grip firm, comforting. "You should stay with Steph and Dave tonight." After a moment, he let his hands drop and he cleared his throat. "Sorry. I don't mean to be bossy. But make sure you get some rest, whatever you decide."

"I will."

By the time Robert dropped her off, she had to drag her aching body into the house. She pulled open the hall table drawer and found a packet of cigarettes – nearly empty, but just one would take the edge off – she chewed at the inside of her cheek. Stuff it. Too tired to actually smoke it. In the pantry she fumbled through the medicine box and found the Panadol, which she popped from the case and downed with a glass of water.

Then, hammer in hand, she checked every room, every door and window. No sign of Ben, thank God. She heaved a sigh, relief flooding her limbs. Hopefully Gerry would have him by now. But she called Steph anyway, and let her friend bring her axe to the house then fuss over her face.

"If he touches you again I'll kill him myself," she said when she finished, dumping the face-washer into the basin. It was tinted pink with her blood.

"Get in line." Lisa managed a small smile.

"I'm dead serious; he's not fooling me again."

Lisa took Steph's hand. "Hey, don't do that. He fooled me too and it's not your fault I hid it. I couldn't have got back on my feet without you."

Steph's jaw was clenched. "I should have seen the signs.

They were there, even in high school."

"Pretty easy to see that now, though. Looking back."

"Maybe. Remember we were in assembly that time, waiting for that guest speaker? The guy from that law firm who stuttered?"

"Dave nearly wet himself."

"Right. But I mean Ben, do you remember what he said?"

"Not really."

"The lawyer was talking about equality in the workplace. Ben said something stupid about a woman's place being to serve her man."

She nodded slowly. He *had* said that. And Dave snickered. And she'd dug her fingers into Ben's thigh. But then, he'd been a kid. It wasn't a sign that he'd become abusive later. "That's a stretch, Steph. Just because he was a typical seventeen-year-old doesn't mean he'd be a pig as an adult."

"Sometimes it does. And he meant it; he delivered it like a joke, but I saw the look he gave you." She squeezed her hand. "When I found you on the kitchen floor in that first place you two had together I thought..."

"I'm sorry, Steph. I should have told you when it started."

"It doesn't matter. You're safe for now – I just don't want to see you like that again."

"I know."

"Get some sleep, all right?"

"I will." She hugged her friend. "Thanks for coming over again. I know you and Dave probably had plans."

She snorted. "Watching a DVD is hardly plans. Dave's fine, don't worry."

"Okay."

Once Lisa set up Steph in the spare room she paused in

the doorway to her bedroom then hauled herself into bed with a sigh.

*

When she woke, the bedroom was bright, stripes of sunlight crossing her dresser, catching on an unused bottle of perfume. It was late then. She dragged herself out of bed and got ready for work. Just one afternoon cleaning job today – a light day, thankfully. Her face was bruised, darkness spreading – and her lip swollen. Classy. Make-up was an option...but who cared? People would ask but she could always lie. Or not; still no idea what to do there.

Steph appeared in the doorway. "I'm running a bit late, so I have to go. How are you feeling?"

"Better I guess." She hugged Steph. "Thanks for staying."

"Anytime. Look after yourself. And let me know when Gerry has that bastard."

"Definitely."

Once Steph was gone, Lisa packed the Holden and headed for Lidelson Real Estate. She barely got halfway through the first toilet stall before her phone rang. She tugged her rubber gloves off and tossed them onto a basin.

It was Gerry. "Lisa, can you meet me somewhere?"

"Yeah, why?"

"We're on Pyke Road and there's been a bad accident. It's...a bit disturbing too, I should warn you."

"Why?"

"It's James Rogers – can you meet us?"

She made to answer but no words would come. Finally, she managed, "Ben's friend Fathead?"

"Yeah. How soon can you be here?"

"I'll leave now. Did you find Ben last night?"

"No, but I will."

Where was the prick? Probably hiding out somewhere.

Or hunting.

Back into the Holden and onto the road again. She rolled the window down, letting the breeze cool her as she tapped a thumb on the wheel in a pattern to rival any thrash band. A bad accident? What had happened to the idiot?

When she pulled into Pyke Road, Gerry's cruiser sat beside an ambulance, which in turn surrounded the purple van, which had hit a tree. No police tape and no urgency to the scene; the ambos were just standing beside their vehicle, talking to one another while Gerry and a man in a suit pointed and gestured.

"Jesus." She strode toward the van and Gerry met her before she reached the driver's door.

"Thanks for coming." A camera with a big lens hung from his neck and sweat beaded at his temples. "I tried Anthony but he must have been in surgery."

"Anthony?"

"I thought he might be able to help explain this," he said. "It's worse than Clint, okay?"

How bad was it? "Okay."

The other man approached. Unlike Gerry, there was no trace of sweat on the man's face – as if for him, it wasn't high summer but a pleasant spring day. He held a pad and pen and gave her a brief smile, his moustache arching around his mouth in a Chopper handlebar. The smile faded when he saw the bruise but he didn't mention it. Instead, he said, "I'm Detective McConnell. Thanks for assisting us. I believe you knew the deceased?"

So Fathead didn't make it. Shit. "I did."

"Well, take a look and tell us what you think, if you don't mind."

She moved around to the driver's side and flinched – Fathead's face was blue and his eyes bulged, but worst of all was the snake wrapped around his neck.

"He's been choked?"

McConnell nodded. "We think the impact came first. He was likely drunk when he hit. It wasn't enough to kill him but the snake seems to have wanted to make sure Mr Rogers died. It bit him and strangled him – before apparently dying itself."

"I...no snake would do that."

The detective gestured to the van. "Care to look again? To be sure."

She turned back and moved a little closer. The van's front end wasn't too badly dented. Fathead was another story.

"It's a red-bellied black snake, right?" Gerry said.

Lisa frowned. He was right. "Yeah." It had coiled itself around his neck twice and now the snake's head dangled over its victim's chest, jaw slightly agape. Two red puncture marks were visible on the back of Fathead's hand. She shook her head. It bit him too? No snake would slip into a car crash to bite and strangle a human.

It simply didn't work like that.

She peered closer. Was the red-belly's head twisted at an odd angle? Like its neck had been snapped?

"Maybe he tried to wring its neck, which is why he was bitten," Gerry said.

"Red-bellies' poison isn't often fatal," she said. "But if it choked him, how did he break its neck? And if he broke its neck first, it couldn't have choked him."

"We're just as confused as you," McConnell said. "But it's useful to have you confirm the likelihood of this being spontaneous."

"So you think it was...what? Staged?"

He gave her an appraising look. "I'm not sure what to think right now. Why do you say that?"

She glanced at Gerry, who said nothing.

McConnell looked to Gerry. "Do I need to know something, Sergeant?"

"There was probably someone else here last night," Lisa said. Things had changed. Leaving the scene of an accident with a fatality, assault, breaking and entering, maybe that was enough to deny Ben bail. "Two more men were in the van."

"It seems so – but how do you know that?" McConnell asked.

She gestured to her lip. "They did this to me before heading this way."

McConnell slipped pen and paper into his jacket then put hands on his hips. "Miss Thomas..." He shook his head. "I think we better head back to the station and have a talk. Sergeant, keep an eye on the scene. Call Officer Johns and tell her once she's done with the notification to get up here." He waved to the paramedics. "Take him."

"Yes, sir."

"Follow in your car, will you?" McConnell said.

She nodded, heading back to the Holden and climbing in. She met Gerry's eyes through the windscreen. He offered a small smile and she tried to return it.

Chapter 13.

Lisa sat at a picnic table behind the station, the shade of an old elm protecting her from the sun. Detective McConnell sighed as he sat across from her. "How are you feeling?"

She raised a hand to her cheek. "It still hurts to talk but I've had worse."

"Sorry to hear that." He took out a cigarette and lit it. A slight breeze tugged at the smoke as he exhaled. She nearly asked for one but decided against it. His Smartphone rested between them, the red light of a voice recorder app on. "So take me back to five years ago."

"Wait – you don't think I killed Fathead, do you?"

He huffed. "I can't really tell until you answer me, but no. I don't. If it had been your ex that turned up dead, then maybe I'd take a look that way. But right now, I just need all the facts."

"And you want to start with why Ben attacked me and Robert?"

"Robert?"

"We volunteer for Lidelson Wildlife."

"I'll need to speak to him too. I assume you can give me his details?"

She nodded.

"All right, back to Ben then. Before the attack – I take it you left him."

"Eventually," she said. "We'd been together since high school..."

He waited.

Lisa looked away as her cheeks grew warm. She clenched her teeth. No. Ben was the one who should have been ashamed. So it took a long time to figure it out? At least she did. Not everyone could say that.

She looked back to the Detective but there was no judgment in his eyes. He simply waited. "It took me a long time to realise he couldn't stop. It was hard to believe he'd changed, by the end, you know? That it wasn't temporary."

"But it wasn't."

"No." She shook her head. "You've probably heard a lot of stories like this. I feel like a bloody stereotype."

"I've heard a few but that doesn't mean yours isn't important – keep going."

She took a stray leaf and tore it in half. Reliving her own stupidity wasn't all that fun but she didn't really have a choice. McConnell had to know what was really going on, shit, maybe he could even help. "Before the real drinking started it was just the weekends. He'd have a big one with his friends, usually after footy. And so did everyone else. It was normal. We were pretty happy I guess. I thought I was lucky – he was good looking and he used to be spontaneous."

"When did it change?"

"He hurt his knee and he couldn't play footy anymore,

so he started drinking a lot. Bigger weekends. I couldn't really keep up so we stopped going out together. Then it was weeknights too."

"And that's when he first hit you, after the injury?"

"No. He got into real estate. Seemed to fit; he could always talk a lot of crap. We started plans to build a house and things turned around for a bit. We had another good year."

"Something changed again?"

"He was still drinking a fair bit but it wasn't until after our finances fell through. We'd already spent a lot of money on the land...it doesn't matter. But that night, after seeing the bank, he got wasted and I told him he was drinking too much and he changed. A bloody Jekyll and Hyde moment; he hit me. That simple." And that easy. It was easy to imagine she could still feel the bump on the back of her head, from where she'd crashed into the table.

"But he apologised the next day. It seemed genuine?"

"Yeah," she said. He knew the patterns, did Detective McConnell. "Didn't happen again for a long time."

He nodded. "What did you do the second time?"

"Stayed with a friend."

"You didn't report it, didn't tell anyone?"

She shook her head. "I told myself the same bullshit; it's temporary, it's just a rough spot, things will get better. Five years ago I decided they never would, and threw him out..."

McConnell waited.

"He'd killed Maggie, my cat. I came home and she was lying in the driveway, her body...broken. He said he was drunk. Angry after one of our fights. Said it was an accident but he wasn't *that* drunk. He never liked her." Lisa made a fist on the table. "Later I changed the locks and dumped his stuff. Told him I never wanted to see him again – I was holding a meat cleaver, so he listened."

McConnell patted her hand. "Good girl. Why did he come back?"

"He's buying a house. I don't know, I thought he might want to try get back together but I told him no."

"How did he react?"

"Anger, drink. And...he got really calm one time too – that was worse, you know? Then he broke into my house and left a letter. I didn't read it."

"You reported this?"

"To Gerry."

"Good. What about last night?"

"We got a call at the Rescue Centre; someone had hit a roo and didn't know how to help the joey."

"So you and Robert left at what time?" He took out his pad. "Habit," he said when she glanced at the Smartphone.

"Probably half past nine. When we got there, there was only the purple van with its lights on and a big grey on the ground before it. He'd been shot."

McConnell checked on his phone a moment. "And the driver?"

"Steve Lindgren. Robert and I asked him what was going on and Fathead...James came out of the dark and attacked Robert with a bat. Ben grabbed me from behind. I knew he was drunk because I could smell the beer on his breath. He hit me a few times. He said he did it because I smashed the windows on his new place."

"I see." He made a few notes. "And you did this after the letter you mentioned?"

"I'd had enough by then, Detective." She flicked the remainder of the leaf aside. "He's been harassing me since he came back. Leaving animal entrails on my front step, the break in, things like that."

"And you reported this behaviour? You're certain it's him?"

"Well I can't prove any of it. But he used to go shooting, when we were together."

"And he brought animals home back then?"

"No. I didn't like him doing it. I refused to let him have any trophies. We used to fight about it actually. It got worse when I decided to volunteer; he thought it was a waste of time."

"But you don't have anything solid to say it was him."

"No. But I spoke to Gerry and he agreed to give Ben a warning. I think that's part of the problem actually." She paused. Was she about to land Gerry in hot water? Couldn't be helped. And he hadn't done anything wrong, not really. "I asked Gerry to warn off Ben when he first approached me last week."

"Go on."

"The animal stuff started then and the break-in followed. Ben reported me for smashing his windows and now he's angry because Gerry hasn't charged me yet."

"Sergeant Hansen hasn't charged you?"

"My dad had just been admitted to hospital – he's still there now. Gerry wanted to give me a break."

"I see. Is your father all right?"

"He fell down some steps. He might have Alzheimer's." There. She'd admitted it aloud. And to a stranger.

His expression softened. "That's difficult for anyone to cope with; you must be under a lot of stress. I hope he's all right."

"Thanks." She met his eyes. "Will Gerry face some sort of...disciplinary measures because of this?"

The detective rubbed at his moustache. "That's not up to me truthfully. Let's go back to Ben. What happened after he hit you?"

"Well, I think it was Fathead that told him to stop but Ben wasn't finished. He showed me more dead roos and said if I told the police, he'd keep killing them. They drove off after that – they were probably all drunk."

"All right, thank you." More scribbling. "What did you do next? How did you get home?"

"Robert drove us. We went to see Gerry. He told us to report it but I decided to sleep on it. Robert wanted to, he was angry, but...I don't want Ben to kill more animals. He's gone crazy, there were roos and a fox. There was even a snake."

His pen stopped. "A red-belly?"

"It could have been – I thought it was a black snake but I wasn't seeing too clearly at the time. Why?"

"And what happened to the animals?"

"We loaded them up and Robert said he'd take them..." She trailed off with a frown. "He wouldn't do that, Detective."

"Don't worry, he'll have a chance to speak to me."

"He was with me, at Gerry's."

"We don't have a complete timeline for the accident yet. He might have taken the snake back and came across Mr Rogers after dropping you off. If he was furious enough, he might have strangled Mr Rogers and used the snake as a bizarre decoy. Or – more likely, as a message. You both care about animals, and in light of Ben's threats, it might not be farfetched at all."

"I don't think Robert bit James, Detective McConnell." It was hard to keep sarcasm out of her voice.

"Nor I." McConnell remained calm.

"Shouldn't you be speaking with Ben and Steve instead?"

"Absolutely. But I need to hear what Robert has to say as well." He switched off the phone's recorder. "And no doubt we'll have to speak again soon. Why don't you go and have something to eat and check on your dad. You've been through a lot."

He was right but she wasn't having lunch yet – she needed to talk to Robert. She stood and the detective walked her through the station, passing Gerry's empty desk with its big St Kilda banner.

Detective McConnell handed her a card with his name and number. "If you need to call. And I don't think I need to say it, but I will anyway; make sure you keep away from your ex."

"I will."

Chapter 14.

Lisa burst into the grain store, grasping at the door as it flew open. She slowed when the customers turned to stare; a farmer and his son, standing beside the chook pellets. She queued up at the counter, waiting behind a woman who was fumbling with her change.

Where was he? Robert was supposed to be at work. Maybe he was in the office or the storeroom. She tapped her foot as she waited. She had to tell him to expect a visit from the detective, but more than that – she had to ask about the snake. Had it been the same snake? Couldn't have been. Impossible.

The woman before her was still struggling with her coins. Lisa smothered a sigh.

The girl at the register called for Robert – the teen must have noticed Lisa's sigh. She gave a rueful smile of thanks and moved along the counter. The door jingled behind her as she waited and she nearly turned to frown at whoever it was. She didn't need a store full of strangers while talking to Robert.

He stepped out of the back room and smiled. "Hey, how are you today?" His own cheek bore a swollen bruise in a mixture of blue and sick-yellow.

"Tired I guess." She paused, glancing at the shop floor. The farmer and his son had reached the counter. "I have to speak with you."

"In private?"

"Yeah. How about the back?"

He shook his head. "We're doing stock-take, it's all hands on deck. Hold on." Robert moved to the door and flipped the 'Open' sign to 'Closed' and nodded to the farmer as the man left. He smiled at the boy, who had the pellet bag on his shoulder and was huffing with the effort.

"Kelli, can you give the others a hand for a moment?"

"Sure."

Once she was gone, Robert leant on the counter. "What's happening? It's not Ben is it?"

"No."

"Have you decided to report him?"

She raised a hand. "Wait, Robert. Something's happened. The police are going to ask you questions about Fathead. He's dead."

"What?"

"He crashed the van last night. I was just there with the police and they think you might have gone back there to strangle him."

"Jesus, why?"

"Because you were angry and because there was a red-bellied-blacksnake tied around his throat. Same as the snake Ben killed, wasn't it?"

"Yeah but that's crazy." Shock covered his face. "And we were together last night, with Gerry. You told them that, didn't you?"

"Of course. But they mean after." She lowered her voice; she'd nearly been yelling. "What did you do with the bodies?"

"I buried the fox and the snake behind the Centre. I was too tired to dig more holes and I didn't want to wake up Anthony, so I left the kangaroos in the ute. They're wrapped in a tarp in the shade. I'm going back at lunch; they probably smell already."

"And you're sure the snake was a red-belly, not a black snake?"

"Red-belly – but don't worry, if the police want to see it I'll just dig it up," he said.

"It would be good if you could." Shoes squeaked as someone moved from the aisles. Detective McConnell. His approach was not hurried, one hand in his jacket pocket, not a single hair out of place on his head. "I'm Detective Andrew McConnell and I'd like to hear your account of last night too, Mr Helmers."

"Let me get someone to mind the counter," Robert said after a moment of confusion, slipping out the back.

Lisa glared at the detective. Was all his understanding before just an act? "You knew I'd come here – you wanted to eavesdrop."

"I would have found him anyway and it sounds like your friend has nothing to worry about."

She folded her arms. "I'm coming."

"Please do."

*

At the rear of the wildlife centre, Robert stood back from the hole – the contents mottled by shade cast from the gum trees. The rich scent of hewn earth filled the air. "See?"

"All right, there's the fox – where's the snake?" McConnell asked.

Lisa peered into the hole. Only the small orange body of the fox was visible, smattered with soil, its black legs like big struck matches. No other black animals were inside and none with red underbellies.

Robert shifted the fox. "It's under the…"

There was only more brown earth.

"Mr Helmers, are you certain this is the correct hole?"

"I only dug one." His eyes were wide and he scraped through the dirt. "This is bullshit, I buried it last night."

"Mr Helmers, I'd like for you to accompany me to the station for questioning at this point."

Robert dropped the shovel. "I didn't kill anyone."

"Tell me about it at the station."

"He didn't do anything," Lisa said. "Anyone could have taken the snake from the grave."

"Did you end up checking on your dad?" McConnell asked. He gestured for Robert to accompany him in his silver sedan – sleek and somehow dishonest.

Lisa exhaled heavily. She hadn't yet. "Do you need anything, Robert?"

"Just let Kelli and the others know," he said. His face was set.

She nodded and strode to the Holden. Inside, she pulled her phone and jabbed at the number for Yarsdale Hospital. The woman on the front desk transferred her to the nurse's station, which at least had good news. He could head home today.

They put her through to her father.

"Dad, it's me. I'm coming to get you now."

"Excuse me?"

"I said, 'I'm coming to bring you home.' Can you hear me okay?"

"Who is this?" His voice was uncertain.

Her heart flipped. "Dad, it's me, Lisa."

"Lisa?" A long pause. "All right. I'll see you soon," he said, and hung up.

What? A lump formed in her throat.

Lisa tossed the phone onto the passenger seat and punched the horn, grinding her fist into the wheel. The horn blared and she let it scream a little longer, before falling back with a sob.

Chapter 15.

Even when she got Dad home that evening, she didn't think he truly recognised her. But he seemed to respond to his possessions. The couch, his radio and the hat hanging off the kitchen chair, even his shoes, which he'd examined while standing in the hall.

She flicked the TV on and helped him into his chair; he was still a little unsteady on his feet, though he wore a somewhat smaller bandage now.

"How about I get something started for tea? Spaghetti bolognaise?" she called from the kitchen.

"That's all right...dear." He said. "I'll be fine."

The hesitation in his voice.

She stopped, hand hovering over a saucepan, shoulders slumped. He still had no idea who she was. The car ride was the same and when he'd stared blankly at her in the hospital...She squeezed the pot's handle. Was he going to remember? Was it already too late for medication? Tomorrow's appointment with Dr Albert couldn't come soon enough.

"I don't mind," she said.

Quiet from the lounge – just the steady prattle of the evening news. She set the pot on the stove and took red mince-meat from the freezer, chucked it on a plate and hit 'defrost' on the microwave. While the mic hummed, she slipped into the study and searched the cupboards. It took a little while, but she soon returned with an old, leather-bound photo album.

She took it to him, opening it at one of her birthday parties as a little girl. "I thought you might like to flip through this while I cook," she said.

"If you like."

She tried to smile. The microwave beeped. "I better check that."

Lisa blinked away tears as she dumped the meat into the pot and hacked at it with a wooden spoon. The sizzle of mince filled the kitchen and she fell into a rhythm. Hack, turn and stir, hack, turn and stir, until the meat browned. Sweat formed at her temples. She drained the fat then added pasta sauce and let it simmer.

Before she put the water on she glanced into the lounge. He was flipping the pages slowly, reaching out to touch some of the photos, mouthing words she couldn't discern.

"Come on, Dad," she whispered, then returned to the meat.

It seemed he remembered little during the meal itself. They ate before the TV – it was like a third person, a blessing, eager to talk and fill every silence between fragmented conversation. She didn't push him and limited her questions to how he was feeling. After tea, she washed up and he shuffled into the kitchen.

"I just wanted to thank you for the great meal," he said, and patted her on the shoulder. She closed her eyes at his hesitant touch, elbow-deep in soapy water. "I think I'd like to lie down now."

He didn't leave. Did he even remember which bedroom?

"Okay. I'll be in the last room tonight," she said. Maybe that was enough of a clue not to upset him.

A moment of silence. "Righto."

His footsteps slipped off down the hall and she glanced after him – his shape was blurred by more tears. She rinsed her hands and snatched a tea towel, wiping her eyes. He had to remember. He had to.

Lisa finished up with the kitchen then moved to the lounge and slumped into his chair. The photo album was open to a page from a few years ago. They stood in front the house, before the new rose bushes, his arm around her shoulder. Both smiling.

She pressed her lips together and closed it before starting to channel surf.

Nothing held her attention. She played games on her phone, checked e-mail, got up to get a drink, then back to the chair where she Googled 'Alzheimer's medication', potency and side effects, brands and costs, until her eyes stung. Half the time she was looking at the wrong pages – overseas costs and brands, and had to start again.

If the medication worked – if he needed it – there was a chance it would be cheaper to buy overseas and ship home.

She massaged her temples a moment. Time for sleep. She locked up before rummaging around for an old nightie in the spare room's dresser, then slumped onto the bed and lay atop the covers. Too hot for blankets – and the ceiling fan didn't work anymore.

How could it have come on so quickly? Her research was limited; she didn't quite know the right questions, it seemed. Did the fall have something to do with it? Or, was this a rough spot, a bump in a slower road to complete loss of memory? A glacial road, if she was lucky, she knew that much. She rolled onto her side.

Somehow, she had to sleep.

*

"Lisa? Lisa, wake up."

She blinked away sleep, rubbing her eyes. "Dad?"

He stood before her in shorts and singlet, his expression concerned. His knees were bonier than she remembered and a large bandage wrapped one calf. "I need you to check something, darl."

Darl? She sprang out of bed. He was back! "What's wrong?"

"I think I might be hallucinating after all that stuff they gave me at the hospital. I got up for a drink and saw something." He frowned. "But I don't know if it's real. It's still dark."

She took his hand. "Let's have a look."

"It's out back."

"All right." She followed him to the sliding door, where he paused. He didn't flick on the outside light. Instead, he parted the venetian blinds and pointed. "There, can you see? Near the paperbark."

Lisa leant close to the glass. Beyond the birdbath,

something big lurked beside the tree, whose pale bark was near-to blue in the moonlight. The figure moved and she gasped.

A white kangaroo.

Easily as big as Pumps had claimed – near to three metres tall. The kangaroo had been grazing on the lawn and its shape seemed to solidify as it lifted its head. The roo towered over most of the garden. Pumps had truly seen her then. She was real.

"Can you see a white kangaroo?" Dad asked.

"Yes," she whispered.

Beside her, he rubbed at his eyes. "I need my glasses. Isn't she too big for a normal roo?"

"I'll check." She reached for the handle. It was waiting for her. She knew it somehow, there was something about the tilt of the head. The kangaroo eyed the house, waiting.

He caught her arm. "Careful. Don't spook her."

Lisa nodded as she slid the door open, stepping onto the verandah and into the warm night. The kangaroo's tail twitched but she didn't run. Lisa crossed the lawn, her bare feet swishing through the grass. Dad watched from the back door.

She paused and looked up to the kangaroo.

Dark eyes regarded her from a large face. No fake roo this time. She was real, magnificent – her tail seemed python-like where it ran along the back fence and her chest broad enough to stop a car, her whiskers silvered and her fur cool white.

A flash of orange crossed the kangaroo's eyes but she made no aggressive move, instead, she lowered her head, lining up a fist-sized eye with Lisa's own. Lisa lifted her hand, hesitating before the kangaroo's face.

Still the kangaroo made no disapproving movement, only the exhale of breath.

Lisa's fingertips brushed the fur and a thunder began in her chest, the thumping of feet striking a grass-plain. The crunch of twigs and leaves, the rasp of bark against fur. There was a sense of movement too, of speed, almost of flight – as if a sudden wind slipped through her hair.

But it faded. The eye widened and within, a grey wall appeared. Smoke. It passed and in its place, a silhouette of a man against white light. A rifle crossed one shoulder and as he walked, a fiery light grew within his stomach. He fell and twisted on the ground, whipping his skull against it, as ears grew from his head. His body shuddered, elongating, legs changing and feet growing until a huge, blood-red kangaroo stood in his place.

Then the white kangaroo blinked.

The images disappeared and Lisa stepped back, mouth agape. What was the kangaroo showing her? A transformation – of who? Smoke and flame too. That wasn't good, especially during bush-fire season.

"What do you want me to do?" She kept her voice soft.

The great white nuzzled her face, just enough for the cool nose to tickle her neck, and then the kangaroo turned toward the fence, and with a single leap, vaulted it as easily as a child stepping over a gutter. No thumping followed her landing, and though Lisa stretched onto her toes – she saw no more.

She turned back to the house.

Dad was wiping his eyes.

Chapter 16.

In the morning Dad seemed all right again, if a little absent-minded. He ended up mixing his years a few times, but at least he knew who she was. Better, but only as good as before the accident. Which was still something.

He didn't mention the great white kangaroo. Maybe he'd forgotten or thought it a dream. She didn't bring it up; best not to trouble him before the appointment. She left him with his scratchings and a promise to be back for the appointment after lunch, then headed down to Lidelson Real Estate to finish up yesterday's job. Old Jameson didn't seem too pleased at her running off yesterday but his grumbling was always good-natured.

And he did provide some information after he finished complaining. Ben had been taken in for questioning while Steve was nowhere to be found. "And young Robert," Mr Jameson continued, his mouth clicking as he spoke, "is apparently still in custody. He needs a barrister, that boy."

Good and bad news – you never got just the good.

As she worked, Lisa found herself staring at whatever lay before her. Door, mirror, bin, whatever. The robot-trance came on too often. How could she concentrate, truly? The white kangaroo was real. Living. Breathing. Unbelievable. And yet Dad saw the roo too – even if there were no tracks in the backyard, there was no denying what happened. Lisa had touched her, seen the vision in her eyes.

The rifle, the terrible transformation, and the ash and fire.

All day she worked with the soft static of the radio but the ABC reported no fires. When was the roo's vision meant to come to pass? Was it even about bushfires? And as for the man with the rifle, it could have been half the men in town – and there was no way to know whether the transformation had already happened. Or was due to happen.

"Why show me those things?" she'd whispered to herself at one point.

If only she could talk it over with someone – but with Dad unwell and Pumps gone, there weren't many people left who'd believe her. Because the farmer *must* have seen the great roo and his attempts to recreate it were because he never saw her again. Which meant...

Lisa lowered her bottle of spray. Frank. The amateur taxidermist – that's why the man had been to see Pumps that day. He'd probably visited the farm a lot during construction of the fake.

How quickly she'd forgotten Frank.

Probably a mistake. Maybe he knew something, could have told her what Pumps saw. Had Frank seen the white roo himself? She had to know. Pumps' last phone call had sounded as if something was amiss. Was it a ploy to get her there? If so, it was a ploy gone wrong.

She had time before the appointment if she skipped lunch.

Lisa finished up, collected her cleaning supplies and practically charged out the doors. "All done," she called to the receptionist.

Lunch traffic slowed her enough that she muttered obscenities at the cattle truck in front of her when they caught a red light. A brown trail of faeces leaked from the truck onto the road and she let the driver pull away when the lights changed.

Out of town, she bypassed Pumps' farm, heading on to Frank's property where she rattled over the cattle grid before pulling up beneath a stand of trees that sheltered the house.

"You better not be working on something," she muttered, looking in Frank's general direction, assuming he was inside.

The taxidermist's place had a 'I'll get around to it' look.

Gutters sagged as if struggling beneath the weight of sunlight. The garden beds overflowed green and a blind in one of the front windows fell from one end. The house lay huddled beyond an old fence-line in the centre of grassy paddocks bordered by dense bush. Not exactly isolated; after all, it only took a few minutes to drive out, but there was no chatter from neighbours like back in town.

Not even the cows grazing in the distance seemed close enough to hear.

She knocked on the front door and waited, eventually knocking again, louder.

Footsteps followed from inside and the door creaked open to reveal Frank's pinched face. His comb-over was the neatest thing about him; his woollen jumper caught with all kinds of bits of fabric and sawdust. He held a pair of glass eyes in one hand, like little pools of black.

"You're one of the Wildlife girls, aren't you?" He licked his lips, glancing over her shoulder. He didn't invite her in.

"Yes, I'm Lisa."

"You need a commission?"

"No." She suppressed a shudder. "It's about Mr Johnson."

Frank clucked his tongue. "Heard about his accident."

"And you were helping him with his...project? The kangaroo?" Somehow she avoided saying 'scam' or 'hoax'.

"I was." His expression hadn't warmed. "Look, I don't think I should talk to you about it." He made to close the door but she caught the edge.

"Could you just tell me what Pumps saw? He thought there really was a giant white kangaroo, didn't he?"

The taxidermist snorted. "He was a good bloke but I don't know if he was all there, if you know what I mean. He thought it came into his garden and showed him something one night. A vision, he said."

"You don't believe him?"

"Sounded like a lot of rot. Smoke and fire and a man turning into a kangaroo or some rubbish. Didn't make sense and I liked his idea about the record book better."

"So he never saw it again?"

Frank grimaced, probably realising he'd admitted to the hoax. "Sorry. I've got something on the stove."

He closed the door.

"Thanks for your help," she said, and headed back to the Holden.

So, he'd been trying to recreate the roo for the hoax, but Pumps had truly seen her. And, she'd shown him a vision. The same vision, it seemed. Why? Something was wrong.

Everything came back to that obvious conclusion. But what exactly?

She checked the time, her watch-face flashing in the sun. Time to get back and take Dad to his appointment.

*

The clinic was running late – well over an hour – she must have tapped a hole in the carpet with her foot, but Dr Albert eventually appeared. His white eyebrows dominated his face, which was mostly unlined.

"Mr Thomas?"

She stood with her father, but he took her arm. "Me first, darl. I'll call you in soon."

"Okay." She sat, moving slowly. Was he ashamed? Or afraid?

When Dr Albert eventually reappeared to call her in, he took her to his dim office and sat her beside Dad, who gave her a smile. It didn't stay in his eyes long.

"Lisa, I understand this might be difficult, but how would you describe your father's health lately? Aside from his fall."

She hesitated before explaining the general memory problems, the trouble he had remembering her after the hospital. He rested a hand on her knee when she described it and the pain on his face was nearly too much. She focused on Dr Albert. "Is that normal? Today Dad seems fine."

"That's certainly true. Lucid states and states of confusion will fluctuate day to day and even moment to moment. Based on what your father has told me, I fear we may be facing a form of dementia known as LBD or Lewy Body Dementia." He handed her a pamphlet. "It's not confirmed and I still want to send him to a neurologist I know in order to be certain. Donald is a friend and we've worked together in the past, be assured that he'll do everything he can."

LBD? Shit. Was that worse than Alzheimer's? The same? "If it is, what does that mean?"

Dad took her hand. "It means I might have five years, sweetheart. Maybe seven, but it could be longer if the drugs work."

That wasn't long enough. She shook her head. "But you might not have it at all, right?"

"Maybe."

She couldn't remember the rest of the appointment.

*

Back at Dad's she started dinner right away. He liked to eat early and she'd skipped lunch, so it was welcome. And she wanted to keep busy.

He joined her in the kitchen.

"How's your head?" she asked.

He raised a hand to the bandage. "Not bad, love. What are you making tonight?"

"Just snags and mashed potato."

"Sounds good." He paused, lifting the pot lid to check on the potatoes. Steam escaped. "Don't be too upset. Life's never easy, not for anyone."

She pressed her lips together. "I can't help it."

He put an arm around her. "I know. We just have to wait and see, all right?"

"All right." She kept her voice steady.

"We'll work it out."

"All right."

"If anyone can, you can. You're a clever girl, you know that?"

A tear escaped and she wiped it away with a small smile. "You've told me before, I think."

"Can I ask you something about last night, darl?"

"The white kangaroo?"

He slapped the table top and he was just like his old self. He was doing better than she was, his grin was wide. "Then I didn't imagine it? Didn't feel like a dream. Too bad we never got a photo – hard to judge, but she was bigger than a normal roo, right?"

"A lot."

"Well, keep an eye out tonight. I'll find the old Canon. See if there's any film left," he said and headed up the passage.

By the time she served up, it seemed he'd forgotten about the camera, though they watched the news together as normal. Toward the end of the broadcast he'd called her 'Annie' again but she said nothing. He remained in high spirits, and it rubbed off a little, which was surprising, all things considered. Compared to the other night – being mistaken for Mum was nothing.

Once again, he headed for bed while she did the washing up – sweating from having her hands in the hot water even with the old air conditioner humming along. When she finished Lisa threw the towel into the washing basket and climbed into the shower. Another long day but thankfully, society had evolved to a point where running water existed.

Before hopping out, she switched the taps to cold and stood under the flow. Almost as good as a swim in the river. She smiled. Hadn't done that in years. And why hadn't she? There was always so much laughter at the river. How many hours had she spent there as a kid during the endless evenings of daylight-saving summers? She'd probably still fit into that old blue one-piece okay but there wasn't really time for much of that anymore. Two jobs, keeping an eye on Dad, trying to deal with Ben, giant white kangaroos – and her most recent hobby – finding dead bodies.

Lisa stepped into baggy shorts and a thin top, checked in on Dad before moving into the kitchen to rummage around in her bag. She pulled out the pack of cigarettes and lighter. Why not? She needed it and just one would take the edge off.

If everything worked out, he wouldn't have LBD.

Or if he did, they could treat it.

Something had to go right soon. It had to. He bloody well deserved it. And she had to stay strong if she was going to help him.

Slipping onto the back verandah, Lisa took the bench seat where she lit the cigarette. A long drag then she leant back to exhale. She took another, glancing around the yard. No moon yet – was it too early for the great white kangaroo to show? Would it even come back? No way to know how many times Pumps saw her. But if the kangaroo did return, Lisa needed to try ask questions. The first visions weren't enough.

Halfway through the smoke, she found a weathered cushion from one of the chairs and put it behind her back, slouching a little. She'd put out the cigarette before she finished; her eyes were growing heavy. She blinked and shifted, trying to get comfortable before settling with a deep sigh.

Something scraped across the lawn.

She straightened, blinking. The moon was up – how long had she dozed?

A dark shape was crossing the lawn from the side of the house – someone had walked up from the street. She stood and the figure flinched.

"Lisa?" It was a man's voice, hoarse.

"Who's there?"

A gasp as the stranger reached for the birdbath, leaning against it. Concrete scraped as the basin shifted on the column. More heavy breathing. Lisa lifted a hunk of firewood from the wood box. "Who are you?" she asked.

"It's...Steve."

"Lindgren?"

"Yes. I...tried your place...guessed you might be here."

"What the hell are you doing?" she hissed.

"Need help...There's something...chasing me, damn it."

"What?"

He groaned. "We fucked up."

She took a few steps forward but didn't leave the verandah. He was holding his stomach as if sick. The moon slid from behind wispy clouds, revealing how pale his unshaven face was. "Steve, what's going on?"

"Ben's...crazy," he said.

"I don't understand – is Ben chasing you?"

"No." He shook his head before more gasps burst free.

Lisa stepped onto the lawn, then froze.

A kangaroo stood in the shadows by the side of the house – near where Steve entered. It waited on hind legs, forepaws still as its eyes glittered. Not the giant white, but a big grey. Lisa opened her mouth when it hopped forward.

"Steve?"

He was shuddering where he stood. He didn't seem to hear her speak.

"Steve, look out!"

The roo kept hopping – fast – and didn't stop when it reached Steve.

It rammed him.

He fell with a grunt, toppling the birdbath, which thumped to the grass. Water sloshed from the heavy concrete basin but it didn't empty.

Steve dragged himself up, twisting back to face her. "Tell it to stop," he cried.

The roo skipped around and kicked him in the ribs, perfectly positioning Steve above the bath. Then it jumped onto his back, reached down and shoved his head into the water with its powerful forearms. Lisa fell back. Steve thrashed and bubbles rose but he couldn't break free. The roo adjusted its grip, holding his face under – as it would a predator in a river.

Steve's thrashing weakened.

He was going to die – just like Fathead. Lisa ran forward and the kangaroo's head snapped up. A low growl rose from its throat. She stopped. The kangaroo continued to growl, only softer now, ignoring the final splashes from Steve as he fell still.

The roo held Steve's head longer, as if to be sure, before finally letting go and leaping free. Muscles rippled beneath fur in the moonlight as it rose tall on hind legs. It surveyed the yard a moment then used its tail to drive off, disappearing the way it came, without a backward glance.

Lisa groaned, wracked by a shuddering so strong she fell

to her knees.
  There'd been a bullet hole in the roo's chest.

Chapter 17.

Lisa led the police into the study so as not to wake Dad. Somehow he'd slept through everything in the backyard and so far, thankfully, he hadn't woken for the aftermath either. None of which he needed to see – like the quiet removal of the body – which hopefully Gerry was able to finish quickly now that the flood-lights were being packed up.

And especially as it turned out that Steve had been eviscerated at some point – just like Clint. Probably why Steve couldn't fight the roo; he was on his last legs.

While Detective McConnell sat at the desk where Lisa paid Dad's bills, she shifted a box of her netball trophies from a stool. The vinyl seat was cool.

"Tell me more about what happened with Steve and the kangaroo."

She gave him a look. "No tricks tonight?" It wasn't that he seemed a bad guy – even with the stunt in the grain store. Shit, he was probably trying to do his job really well. And protect people. Just two of the justifications she imagined he'd bring out if she asked but which he didn't offer.

No. Maybe he felt just as powerless as she did. How was anyone supposed to stop animals that came back from the dead to commit murder? Because she hadn't imagined that bullet hole. The blood made a black hole in the roo's chest. It paused in the moonlight, she'd had a good look.

It was one of the ones Ben shot.

"You're clenching your fists," McConnell said.

She relaxed her hands in her lap. "Not my ideal Friday night."

"What upset you?"

"You know what happened. I thought you'd have arrested me by now actually."

He set his pen and pad aside and leant forward, suit jacket falling open. "I don't like to make arrests without proof. I have to admit, at first glance you look good for this one. You've been involved in all the deaths around these parts in the last week or two – how many bodies have you found recently?"

"Three. You found James."

"Right. And Mr Healy's wounds are very similar to the ones found on Mr Lindgren. Robert and your ex confirmed the assault story, so that's motive for tonight and James Rogers. Your knowledge of the area and animals, maybe that's means and you certainly had the opportunity to kill these men." He leant back. "But I'm not convinced just yet."

She straightened a little. "Why not? You believe me, about the kangaroo?"

He shrugged. "I actually grew up on a farm behind Melbourne. I once saw a kangaroo drown a dingo in a dam, so on one hand I don't think it's stretching the limits of plausibility."

"But?"

"But on the other, some of the most duplicitous crimes are tough to prove simply due to that very fact. And the wounds in his stomach do support a roo attack. There's evidence in the grass that suggests a large animal was on the property. Only, who's to say you didn't find Mr Lindgren wounded and finish him off? A struggle at the birdbath? It's a big enough basin – what, six inches deep? Easily enough to drown a man."

"I'm to say."

"Of course." He smiled as if to draw attention to the absurdity of such a response, as far as the law was concerned.

"I'm not going to commit murder while my dad is sick. He needs me."

"He does."

She sighed. How could she do that? No-one was going to believe her if she said the kangaroo that committed the murder was dead. "I don't think either of us can prove anything tonight."

He crossed his legs at the ankle. "To be honest, Miss Thomas – that's true. But you're still going to have to either come with me to the station to face charges or try and convince me. Right now."

"Who's going to look after my father if you lock me up?"

He raised a hand. "Slow down. Think about yourself for a minute too. Is there anyone who can prove that you didn't drown Steve Lindgren?"

"I don't think the neighbours saw anything, it's late."

He sighed. "All right. Can you call someone to come over, while you're at the station?"

"I'm being arrested?"

"On suspicion of the murder of Steve Lindgren."

She folded her arms, shaking her head. McConnell waited. Damn it all. Finally, she stood. "Let me get my phone. I'll call Steph."

*

Lisa paced the concrete floor of her cold cell while Gerry and McConnell spoke in the office, their voices hushed. She'd been questioned again by McConnell, this time on tape, and returned to the cell.

The possibility of being charged with murder hovered over her, and it was dead serious, and yet – what about Dad? Was he okay? She had to check on him. Were Steph and Dave all right? God, would he even remember them?

Gerry left the office and walked over, pausing at the bars. "How are you going? Want coffee or something?"

"That'd be good. Gerry, can you check on Dad?"

"Will do."

"So, what's happening now?"

He exhaled heavily. "This isn't the sort of thing I deal with a lot, you know? Been here all my life, same as you, and twelve years with the police already but the only killings we've had since then were road accidents. This feels different. It feels wrong, even for murder."

She nodded; he was right about that.

"McConnell's calling the shots, but you'll probably be released without charge. I'm trying to convince him you don't pose a threat to Ben."

She reached through the bars and took his hand. "Thank

you." She paused, looking up at him. "How come you believe me?"

He met her eyes. "I just know you wouldn't do that stuff."

"Sergeant." Detective McConnell moved to the cell and Lisa withdrew her hand. "I'm releasing you, Miss Thomas. I still expect you to stay in town until this business is resolved, understood?"

"Understood."

"And make sure you look after your father," he said, then motioned to Gerry as he walked back out.

Gerry unlocked the door and escorted her outside to the cruiser. "To your dad's?"

"Yes, thank you. How's Robert?"

"Angry. He's got the same conditions as you."

Lisa made a fist in her lap, fingernails biting into her palm. Hopefully Gerry wouldn't see it in the dark. "We have to find out what's going on."

"We will," Gerry said.

"Ben's out, isn't he?"

He hesitated. "He has a court date."

"That's not much of a comfort."

"I know, I'm sorry."

"Not your fault. What did he say?"

"Not much, the prick."

"Steve was afraid of him, you know. At the end, he said that Ben was crazy."

Gerry glanced at her. "He's on really thin ice, Lisa. And he's going to do time, I promise you that."

"Yeah." She turned to the dark beyond the passenger window. Was it unfair to expect Gerry to uncover the truth behind the killings? And yet – maybe they would stop soon anyway. With Ben. If the animals he and the others murdered were coming back for vengeance, then Ben would be the last one. Bizarre? Definitely. But it made sense; it was almost logical.

And it would no doubt land her a life sentence.

Then who would look after Dad?

Could the giant kangaroo help? Did any of it relate to the man with the rifle? She was essentially blind, floundering from one disaster to another. One supernatural nightmare to another.

But all that would change tomorrow.

Tomorrow she'd do something herself. Find Ben and put a stop to the madness. She'd warn him somehow, force him to leave town, even. She nearly scoffed. Fat chance he'd listen. But she had to try.

Alone, even if it wasn't smart. No-one was going to understand why she had to do it. Robert was out of the question and so was Gerry. McConnell wouldn't have a problem reading something iffy into either choice.

That left Steph and her wood splitter.

Lisa stared ahead. She'd be at Dad's soon enough and she could ask.

Chapter 18.

"Has he been up?" Lisa asked the moment she set foot inside the front door.

In the lamplight Steph switched off the TV and rose, swatting at Dave's hand when he gave her backside a slap. He grinned and ran a hand over his shaven head as if suddenly embarrassed.

Steph glanced up the dark passage, keeping her voice low. "He woke not long after you left. We told him you were helping the police with an attempted break-in. He was a bit worried but he went back to bed."

"Thank God. Did he recognise you?"

"Dunno about me," Dave said. "But he knew who Steph was."

"Don't worry about your dad for a minute. He's fine, honey." Steph raised an eyebrow. "What about you? Did you get charged?"

"No. But it could get worse – I think something's going to happen to Ben next. And if it does, Detective McConnell won't have any more doubts."

"Is something going to happen to Ben?" Steph asked.

"I don't know." Lisa took a seat. She hadn't told them all the details about Steve, but they knew the circumstances around Fathead – the whole town would have by now. "Steve had been cut open by claws – same as Clint."

"Jesus," Steph said, her eyes wide. "You think there's a feral animal loose?"

"Maybe."

Dave shook his head. "Slow down, you two. No feral animal's gonna lie around the place waiting to slash into people. It's a person trying to make it look like an animal. Like Robert maybe."

Lisa frowned. "Robert? Why?"

"Well, he's not really a local, is he?" he said with a shrug. "Could be him."

Steph snorted. "Don't be an idiot."

"I don't think Robert did this, Dave." Lisa stood again. "Thanks for coming over tonight. I owe you both." She hesitated, looked from face to face. Steph deserved a break yet Lisa had to ask for more help. "Actually, I think I need another favour. Well, two more."

"Work tomorrow?"

"No, I want to go and warn Ben. Wanna load up your axe and come with me?"

"No way," Dave said. "I'll come, but Steph ain't going near that piece of shit."

Steph rolled her eyes.

"Really? Thanks, Dave," Lisa said. "Can I pick you up from the shop first thing?"

"I'll be there."

"What about the other favour?" Steph asked.

"Do you know any home-care nurses?"

She gave a slow nod. "Maybe. Rhonda used to do it full time. But she's cut back. I can ask."

"Great. Tell her I'll pay."

"You want her here tomorrow morning then?"

"If she can."

"Well, I can check on your dad if Rhonda's busy so don't worry."

Lisa hugged her, blinking back tears. "You're too good to me."

"I know." She smiled. "Now get some sleep."

Lisa let them go then locked up, checking the door twice. Then she looked in on her dad again, he was snoring, so she headed for the shower. The cell hadn't been filthy but the concrete was stained with a variety of shades she didn't care to analyse. Then it was straight into bed – tomorrow was probably going to be another big day.

Would the animals hold off until then?

She'd have to risk it. If she didn't get some rest she'd only fall asleep at the wheel.

*

Dave was waiting at the cafe when she pulled up, sitting at one of the steel-framed outdoor tables with his feet up on the opposite chair. The early morning light reflected off the glass table-top and she rolled forward to dodge the light.

She waved and he hopped in. "Did you meet Rhonda yet?"

"Yeah. She seems great." An older woman, she wasn't

dad's age but her no-nonsense attitude reminded her of him. In any other circumstance they probably would have been friends.

"Steph thinks so. Personally, I think she's a bit opinionated."

"Really?" Lisa had to smile.

"Yeah. Anyway, about Ben. Think he'll be at his new place or his parents' joint?"

"I'll try Overlook Boulevard first."

"Right."

Lisa wound through the streets, passing young parents with prams, kids on skateboards weighed down by their backpacks and folks just out for a walk in the sunshine. How lucky they were to have so little to worry about. Or so it seemed. Who knew what was going on below the surface? Routine was a pretty good mask when you got down to it.

When she pulled up at the house it was clear no-one was around. No car, no signs of movement within. The broken windows had been replaced, with masking tape 'X's on new glass.

"Off we go then," she said.

Dave rested his arm on the window. "Nervous?"

"I guess. Angry too."

He nodded. "So, did you kill Steve or what?"

She glanced at him. Typical, tactless Dave. "No, Dave. But thanks for asking."

"Just wanted to check. No-one thinks you did it. Well, me and Steph don't anyway."

Her foot lifted off the pedal a little. "People think I did it?"

"Don't slow down," he said. "Maybe. Had Ronnie come and ask me about it when we were opening up today. I think he just wants to get the goss. But you gotta admit, it doesn't look that good."

"No, it doesn't." Was she the talk of the whole town?

"Well don't worry, it'll get sorted."

"Yeah?"

"Yep. Karma and that."

She had to smile. "Hope it gets its butt into gear then."

Trees rose up around the road as they headed out of town, bypassing Swallow's Road and closing in on homes with a bit of land. Not quite on tank water, but far enough out that it would have been peaceful year round.

The Drummond property was a big mud brick place set off the road and obscured by scattered gums. A winding driveway led to a miniature roundabout that hugged the big owl sculpture in the centre of a rose patch. The sun flashed off mirrors spread across the mosaic bird as she and Dave approached the front door. Currawongs chatted in the trees above.

She pressed the bell and stood back.

"What if he's not here?" Dave asked, stretching his arms behind his head.

"I rang his phone before picking you up and there was no answer. Maybe his mum will know."

"Press it again," Dave said.

"Give them a minute."

"Nah, let 'em know we're in a hurry." He leant in and jabbed the bell.

The door opened.

Ben stood in the arch, a deep frown on his face. Unshaven, his hair was a mess and he wore ripped jeans, a black Bonds shirt but no shoes. The jeans had a red stain at the cuff, as if he'd cut his leg. "What do you want?" He folded his arms over his chest. His nails were coated in dirt.

"To speak to you. It's important," she said.

"Oh? Now it's important. That's hilarious." He glanced at Dave, who was grinning at the taller man. "And what the hell are you smiling at, Clarke?"

"Just thinking about that time I beat you up in high school," Dave said.

Ben spat into a nearby pot plant. "Want to try again?"

"Any time you're up for a challenge, mate – but it's not like picking on women, just so you know. Maybe you better hit the weights first? I can come back."

Ben snarled, his face flushed.

"Stop it," Lisa shouted. It was nice to have Dave along but damn he was relentless with his shit-stirring. Not that Ben didn't deserve it.

Dave raised his hands and Ben exhaled through his nose. "Fine. What do you want?"

"I want to warn you. This stuff that's happening, it's getting worse. You know what happened to Steve and James?"

His eyes narrowed. "I heard."

"Who's to say you're not next?" she asked. "Maybe you should take a holiday or something."

"Worried that Detective McConnell will pin it on you if something happens to me?"

"Just be careful." No way was she going to let him draw her out on that one.

"Maybe I should get a new rifle for protection?" A faint smile crossed his lips.

"What?"

Dave put a hand on her shoulder. "Let's go. He's had his

warning."

Lisa stared at Ben. Had there been emphasis on the word 'rifle' or did she imagine it?

"Goodbye, Lisa." Ben closed the door, giving it a shove when it popped back open. The click of a lock followed.

Lisa let Dave pull her to the Holden but once inside, she didn't start the car right away. She fiddled with the keys, staring up at the house. Why did he have to keep stirring her up? Such a prick. And did he even care that two of his friends had died?

"Let's go," Dave said. "My customers will wither and die without me."

She shook her head as she fired the engine and pulled around the owl sculpture. "He didn't seem worried, did he?"

"Arrogant prick, that's why."

"Maybe." Could it be that simple?

"Should've let me flatten him for ya. After all the shit he put you through."

"Let's just go."

At the bottom of the drive she paused. McConnell lurked within his silver sedan, but made no move to follow when she turned back toward town. She thanked Dave and dropped him off before heading to her first job – only Mrs Ascot tittered on her way out of the front door, making an excuse about things being 'a bit tight this week' and rushing down the driveway, nearly jerking her son's arm out of its socket as she did.

Lisa frowned after the car. "Nice to have the benefit of the doubt."

The rest of the day's work passed without any more last-minute cancellations. Before heading back to Dad's, where she'd finally relieve Rhonda, she checked on her place. The afternoon sun streaked across the front garden, colouring the leaves into orange flames.

No-one seemed to have been inside and there were no animal corpses in the backyard. She watered the plants – even the agapanthus appeared unhappy – then wheeled the bins down to the driveway and wrangled them onto the nature-strip and stood back.

Would Ben survive whatever was happening? Would he come after her again? So much for getting answers; so much for taking matters into her own hands. She was still in limbo, with McConnell on her case, Ben menacing, the mystery of the white roo unsolved and Dad in trouble.

What now? Mum would have rolled up her sleeves.

"Me too, then."

She'd make sure Dad was okay and she'd keep going. What else was there to do?

Chapter 19.

Two blocks from Ronald Street, Lisa slammed on her brakes.

A car beeped its horn behind her but she ignored it.

The white kangaroo stood on its hind legs in the middle of a zebra crossing, staring right at her. An ear twitched as it watched.

Two kids rushed up to the crossing and paused, glancing at her car before charging directly through the kangaroo. She blinked. Once they'd crossed, they continued up the street without a backwards glance. The kangaroo began to dissolve – reappearing at the end of the block beside a pair of elms.

Another blast from a horn.

In her mirror, a woman was waving her arms from inside her Jeep. Lisa motioned for the driver to go around. She ignored the shout as the woman roared by.

A spirit? The roo had been flesh and fur on her last visit, what had changed? Lisa closed her eyes and took a deep breath. When she opened them, the roo was still there. She eased her foot onto the accelerator and the car crept forward. At the end of the block, near the park, the roo dissolved again only to reappear further along, this time beside a squat red post box sheltering beneath a row of spiky bottlebrush. Her pulse quickened; it wanted her to follow. She trailed it to the edge of town before pulling off the road – Dad. She grabbed her mobile and rang Rhonda.

"Hi Rhonda, it's Lisa. How is he?"

"A bit agitated because he can't remember his TAB account number but other than that he's fine."

"Good. I know it." She gave the number while keeping an eye on the roo where it waited on the road. A removalist truck passed through the pale animal. "I'm sorry to ask at such late notice, but I'm in a bind and I can't get home yet. Any chance you could stay longer?"

"I can but I'll have to charge you a fair bit for the honour."

Damn. But she couldn't lose the kangaroo; not now. And ringing someone else might take time and Rhonda was already there. "I understand. And thank you; I might be a few hours."

"No problem."

"Thanks." She hung up and resumed her hopscotch-like chase. The further out of town Lisa drove, the longer the gaps between appearances. Swallow's Road twisted and she lost sight of the roo, but around the next bend and there she was, sometimes turning to hop into nothingness and sometimes just standing motionless before dissolving into the wall of bark and leaves.

When the roo appeared at Anne's Lane, the turn for Pumps' farm, Lisa slowed. Where was the white kangaroo going? There was nothing at his house, surely. She bumped up the gravel road and crunched to a stop before the farmhouse.

The roo stood by the still-unfinished fence.

Lisa grabbed her phone then opened the glove box, scrambling around for the Maglite – if she was going to end up in the bush alone in the dark, it'd be nice to have the kind of torch that was heavy enough to double as a weapon. Just in case.

"Where are we going?" she asked the kangaroo as she approached.

It faded away.

Not much of an answer. She slipped around the fencepost and climbed through the undergrowth, coming across the same trail she'd found when Pumps first called. She followed it deeper. All around, stripes of dying light coloured the bush – bark blushed a pinkish orange while the ground lay heavy with new shadow.

But the kangaroo appeared in the distance, towering over a fallen log. She slipped between two messmate onto another path, trailing the kangaroo into the darker parts of the bush. Light faded but she didn't need the torch yet; climbing over the log, whose colour had been leeched to grey, a clearing stretched before her.

Grass and weeds spread across the open space, lit by the last of the sun.

The roo stood in the centre in a patch of bracken, scratching at the ground.

Lisa moved closer, feet crunching twigs. The kangaroo disappeared before she reached the point where the ground should have been torn – but the earth was undisturbed. The kangaroo was a white sliver between distant trees.

"Where are we going?"

Lisa walked on, torch in hand. At one point she paused to wipe her brow and temples. The evening was barely cooler than midday and the longer she walked the further behind the farm fell. Could she find her way back? She had the Maglite at least.

By the time she neared the roo for what had to have been the tenth time, it was dark enough that she had to choose her steps carefully. The kangaroo had become a grey smudge. It had stood on the edge of another path – only when she reached the spot where it disappeared did she find a broader way, not a narrow animal trail. The dirt was looser, almost a silken grey in places. Few weeds grew across it and she nodded to herself when a smooth bump appeared in the road – a ramp or a 'jump' as she used to call it as a kid.

Not that she was a great rider or anything, but it was clearly man-made.

A dirt bike trail; the Dump Track it used to be called, named for its proximity to an old illegal rubbish tip.

The kangaroo hopped along, pausing frequently to check Lisa was following. She clicked the torch on and continued. The beam cut through the shadows and when it passed over the kangaroo dark holes appeared – revealing the bush beyond.

It kept hopping and still Lisa found herself unable to close the distance but she never lost the roo either. The Dump Track wound through the bush, sometimes veering off into secondary paths – one of which the white kangaroo chose.

When she reached the fork the kangaroo was gone.

Lisa let her torch range ahead. The trail curved around a dense stand of trees, eventually rejoining the original road. Lisa paused, running the torch across the huddled trunks, peering between them. No sign of the roo.

"Where are you?" she called.

Was she supposed to go on? She took a few steps forward then stopped. The whole time the kangaroo – or its spirit – led her, it made sure she didn't fall behind. What had changed?

Maybe the side path was the way.

She moved along her back trail, torch beam crawling over tree trunks and dirt. Only her own footprints until... another branch to the path – driving into the trees and half-concealed by a build-up of dirt, weeds and saplings.

There was the smell of dead animal to the air.

A chill crossed her shoulders, like icy fingers against her skin. Something was wrong. Had Ben been here? She wheeled on the bush. Was he here now? No. Only shadow between the leaves. Shit. Maybe she'd made a mistake, coming alone. Chasing a spectre.

Lisa turned back to the path, squinting past the beam of light.

Something red lay beyond the screen of branches. She moved closer and pushed through. A small path led to a red door set into the earth, which looked to have half-buried a shelter. Trees and brush grew thick on the sides and over the top of the door. Weeds hung like an errant fringe.

Her grip on the torch tightened as she reached out to run her fingers across the bolts in the steel door – even they were covered beneath the heavy red paint. Bright, like a fire truck. Faint words crossed the surface but none were legible. Was it a fire shelter? A bomb shelter from the war? Unless…no, Dad had told her about an old depot for storing dynamite, once used for road construction. Is this what the kangaroo wanted her to find? What waited inside?

There was no handle on the door, only a pair of holes, one set above the other and she had no key.

Lisa stepped closer, running the torch along the edges. It was ajar. She cinched the Mag beneath her arm and dragged the door open with a grunt. Darkness and the scent of animal. And death. She moved deeper into the shelter, feet shifting over the sandy floor, torchlight forging ahead. A large shape rested at the limit of the light, where the shelter opened. Lisa's steps faltered when she neared.

White fur.

Sand flew as she ran forward, collapsing by the head; the kangaroo lay on the floor, its neck twisted. "No." The roo's dark eyes were open. A trail of blood had trickled from beneath the body, eaten up by the sand. There was no breath in her chest. The stillness of the shelter was heavy; Lisa's shoulders slumped.

"You bastard, Ben." Somehow, it was Ben. He was the man with the rifle, he was the one who'd shot the giant white kangaroo. She couldn't prove it but that didn't matter. His grin, when he mentioned 'rifle' at the house. It was him. Had to be.

Her fist ached where she gripped the torch. How dare he? He'd murdered the most beautiful animal she'd ever seen. A gentle creature – maybe even ancient, sacred. And now she was gone, smothered in the dark, her life wasted by that fucking bastard!

Lisa drew in a shuddering breath.

"Damn you." Anger wasn't enough; it didn't help anyone. Wouldn't change what had happened. And yet, the smouldering rage burned tears away. She drew out her pouch of salt and sprinkled it over the body, then added some more – everything she had, shaking the little bag over the fur.

"Watch over her."

But who would watch over the white roo? Maybe the white kangaroo was the one Lisa had been praying to in the past, the one who'd watched over all the other animals. A moment of quiet would be fitting. Of darkness too. She flicked the torch off, leaving only her breathing.

A pale glow.

Was the torch broken? No – the glow came from the roo's head. Lisa leant down. Light flickered in one of the roo's eyes, resolving into the image of a brilliant owl, blinding white. The eye blinked. Now running water rushing over sand and smooth rocks, its clarity gradually being overtaken with blackened leaves and ash. Another blink. When the dark eye reopened, the Wildlife ute sat in a clearing. A dark shape slammed into it, appearing from nowhere. The ute tipped but didn't fall, wheels stirring dust when it thumped down again. Two figures sat inside, waving their arms.

One more blink and now the eye revealed a paintbrush.

And then only a soft dark.

Chapter 20.

On the way back her phone beeped. A voice message – shit, was it Dad? Reception was patchy. She crashed through the last of the bracken, boots scraping across the gravel driveway, torch beam wild, and leapt into the Holden.

Rhonda. Dad was in hospital again.

Lisa jammed the key into the ignition and stomped on the pedal, tearing down Pumps' drive, scorching the night as she flew along the black highway.

By the time she reached Yarsdale Hospital visiting hours were far beyond over. But at the dim-lit nurses station one of the women let her look in on him, once again propped up on white pillows, his face calm as he slept to the blip of the heart monitor. It seemed strong enough.

On the way to the hospital, ghostly trees and reflectors flashing by on the roadside, she'd played Rhonda's message half a dozen times. He'd collapsed in the bedroom. Rhonda had heard, and when she couldn't wake him, had the ambulance on the way in seconds. That was all Rhonda knew. "You're welcome to call me if you need to, dear," her message said. Lisa had wanted to thank her, but there was time for that later. And better to let Rhonda rest; she'd given up a lot already.

Lisa turned back to the nurse who stood beside her in the darkened hospital. "But you don't know what's wrong?"

"I'm sorry, Miss Thomas. It could be a lot of things – even a reaction to the medication we're giving him. We're waiting on test results. There's nothing you can do tonight."

"Okay." She stared at a novelty pen on the desk. It had a stupid, gleeful face. "I guess I'll go home."

"We'll call you in the morning." The short woman paused, then reached out to pat Lisa's hand. "You look pretty stuffed. Did you want to take a powernap before you leave?"

"Maybe some coffee?"

"I got lots of that."

Much later it seemed, she was climbing into her own bed after having locked up and checked the house twice, forcing herself to be sure about the doors and windows. And now there was only the pillow and the cool sheets, the 'underneath everything else' hum of the air-conditioner.

*

Lisa rolled onto her back and stretched like a starfish.

The sun was out there somewhere, but it didn't matter yet. Just for a moment, she could lie still and not have to get up to help anyone.

Dad.

She groaned. "Oh God." What kind of daughter was she? To enjoy the thought that – even if only for a little while – he was under someone else's care. And maybe it was the best place for him, but just as likely; maybe not. She'd sure as shit never decide lying in bed.

And the vision from the white kangaroo.

The ashes in water – the aftermath of a fire? It clearly linked to the fire she saw during the first vision. And the paintbrush...well, didn't that mean her father? But why? And the ute was a clear warning. Something dark was attacking it, something powerful enough to rock the whole vehicle.

Finally, there'd been a blinding-white owl. As if it was covered in mirror-pieces, like a mosaic? She sat up. Ben's house. Ben. It all came back to Ben.

Lisa flung the sheet aside and ran for her phone. Nearly flat. "Damn." She plugged it in and fumbled through dishes on the bench until she found Detective McConnell's card. She dialled and tapped a bare foot on the cool tiles.

"Detective McConnell speaking."

"Detective? It's Lisa Thomas, I need your help."

"Is there something you'd like to tell me?"

"Yes. I think Ben is behind everything that's happening. I want you to come with me when I go and confront him at his parents' house." No taking chances and no being fobbed off this time either. She'd kick the damn door in.

"I wouldn't advise that."

"I could use a reliable witness."

Silence followed. "That's just not a good idea, I'm afraid."

"Fine. At least you know where I'll be." She hung up, changed her top then stepped into her jeans. "Come on, come on," she said, pulling the laces on her boots tight. Straight into the Holden and out of town, along the outer roads and then she was turning up toward the mud brick property and its owl statue.

Killing the engine, she took a deep breath then popped the boot and got out. The sun beat down on her head and shoulders and she wiped her face. Only mid-morning and it was already too damn hot. Inside the boot, she pulled up the lining and lifted the tyre iron from atop the spare but paused with one hand on the lid. The rumble of a car engine.

Down on the road, a silver car sped toward the turn into the Drummond property. She glanced at the house. No movement in the windows, no-one came to the door. McConnell was winding up the driveway.

The wheels soon ground to a halt before her.

"You need to get back into your car, put that down and head home," he said once he stepped out. As before, his composure defied the elements; no sweat, no flushed face, nothing.

"Thanks for coming. I think Ben's lost control." She strode toward the front door.

"Lisa."

She thumped on the door. "Ben? Ben – get out here and..." The door swung open. Dirt was strewn across the hallway. Beyond, a houseplant lay in a shattered pot on dark slate tiles.

"Miss Thomas, you can't –" McConnell stopped beside her.

"If he's in there I want to know," Lisa said. "He's the one who did all this."

His frown was fleeting. "You think Ben killed all those people?"

"He's involved."

Detective McConnell moved around Lisa and into the

house. "Mr Drummond? Are you all right?"

Lisa followed him down the hall. Family portraits hung on the wall in ornate frames. Full of smiling people. She stopped, taking one down with a wordless murmur. She and Ben at a party, both laughing, both with drinks in their hands and the rainbow wreckage of a party popper in her hair. Was it sweet or sad that they'd kept the picture?

"Miss Thomas?"

She returned it and joined Detective McConnell in the kitchen. On the table a place had been set for one – but the plate was covered in grass. Animal droppings littered the chair.

Her stomach twisted. "What's going on?"

"I have no idea," he said. The detective peered over the kitchen sink and his lip curled.

"What is it?" she asked.

"Blood."

In the sink, a shallow pool of blood. What had stopped up the drain? "Human?"

"I don't know." He drew a gun from beneath his jacket. "Something is going on here, you're right about that. Might be safest if you stay close to me now."

Carpeted steps led up to the second storey. Detective McConnell started up but Lisa paused by the door beneath the stairs. A heavy table and an armchair had been placed against it. Something...wrong spread from beyond the door. Where was Ben? Where were his parents? Away? On holiday as usual?

She took the arm of the chair and hesitated.

"Miss Thomas?"

She flinched.

"Lisa. Can you join me up here." It wasn't a question, and his tone suggested more unpleasantness.

Up the stairs and onto the landing where McConnell stood before Ben's old room. Further down the hall waited a closed door with a tassel hanging from the handle – his parents' room. A hall table had been dragged across the doorway and a heavy statue from the yard outside rested before it, a great concrete Buddha, his smiling face oddly complacent in the quiet – a quiet which grew more unnatural the longer she stood in the Drummond home.

"What is it?"

He stepped aside. "Animals have been here."

Ben's room was a converted exercise space, but the treadmill had been knocked into a window; shattered glass piled on the dark carpet below like sharp ice. A blowfly buzzed in through the gap, a dull sound adding to chaos. It flew to a fluoro pink mat on the floor, coming to rest on a clot of blood and hair.

Dark hair, not white.

More blood spots and smears were visible in the room – along with scars in the carpet, as if torn by claws. A smear of blood crossed the mud brick walls, spanning a vintage Coke poster down to the skirting board.

Yet it didn't seem like enough blood to prove a death. "How much blood would indicate a murder?"

He ran thumb and forefinger over his moustache. "More than this. But it appears to be another attack." He glanced at her a moment. Was he thinking about Steve and the fountain? Or Fathead in his van?

She returned the look. "Think I'd do this then call you over to 'discover' it with me?"

"You said you wanted a reliable witness."

"Then I'm a master criminal doing hard drugs to stay awake – because I spent most of last night with Dad in the hospital." Not a complete lie.

His expression softened but he shook his head. "Look, you have to know that –" He stopped, turning to the window. "I smell smoke."

"Fire?"

He glanced over his shoulder before turning back to the window. "You haven't heard? The forecast is bad. Not Black Saturday bad – but we need to check." He started down the stairs and Lisa hurried after, rushing from the house. In the driveway, she spun a circle. Smoke pumped into the sky like an ugly grey worm, looming over the hills in the distance. "How close is it?"

"Come on." He strode to his car and switched ABC radio on. The announcer was finishing a list of places at risk. "... and finally, people in areas surrounding Yarsdale are advised to monitor news outlets for incidents involving the fire in the Alpine National Park." Detective McConnell turned it down but didn't switch it off. He reached for his police radio and called the station.

"Lidelson Station."

"Karen, it's Andrew McConnell. What's the latest?"

"Nothing new. CFA's still doing last minute back-burning." Her voice crackled over the speakers. "We could use a hand down here, actually."

"What's wrong?"

"The Browns and the Healy boys are getting into it. Gerry's trying to calm them down but it's going to turn bad. I can tell."

"I'll be there soon." McConnell's expression was clouded with worry as he stared across the hills to the plume of smoke.

Billy Brown was an idiot – and so were Clint's sons, it seemed. But then, she could hardly blame them. Any of them.

"Do you have family around here?" she asked.

"No – but you know how these fires can change direction. If it's in the park now, it could easily run down toward Mansfield. My mother is in a home there."

"Oh."

"You should go home and keep the radio on. And no more stunts like this," he said, removing his jacket and tossing it on the passenger seat, his shoulder holster dark against his shirt.

"So you do think I had something to do with all that inside?"

"No idea what to think anymore." He rolled back his sleeves, part of an apparent concession to the heat, then hopped into the car and backed onto the grass, turning toward town. Lisa glanced to the smoke. He was right – distant yes, but fire moved when the wind got behind it.

She tilted her head as something moved at the treeline, just beyond the yard. A dark figure stepped out then ducked back in. As if hiding. She took a step closer, shielding her eyes with a hand. No movement now. Was it Ben? Was he hiding out there in the trees?

The tyre iron had grown slick. She wiped her hands on her jeans then squeezed the steel tight. It had to be him. He'd heard the car when she arrived and ran out back.

Lisa took a few more steps toward the edge of the yard.

If she ran, could she catch him? If he lurked in the trees and if it was Ben...did she want to? Hard to forget the blood in the sink. And the marks in the exercise room or the sense of wrongness from beneath the stairs.

Despite Detective McConnell's warning...she'd come for answers. The white roo showed her the owl for a reason. There was something to be discovered here. And there was that faint smile too, when Ben mentioned getting a new rifle. Lisa clenched her teeth. Her heart rate was up. Just go. Get on with it, Mum would have said. She set off at a run, tyre iron swinging.

The treeline loomed before her, shadows thick between the trunks. She leapt over a sharp depression and detoured a young fruit tree before skidding to a halt at the barbed-wire fence. Was this the spot where the figure appeared? She pushed on the wire where the tension lagged and climbed through the fence, stepping into the trees.

Shade cloaked her. The crunch of bark underfoot filled the bush. The scent of hot gum leaves; it should have been wonderful. No birds sang. No sign of a dark figure, not even a sense that anyone had set foot within the trees recently. No crushed leaves on the ground, no bent saplings. Deeper into the trees the shadows stood thicker, sound grew duller. Was there a slight hiss of breath back where the dark was so profound? The image of a kangaroo, fur matted with blood, flashed in her mind. Had he been killing more?

Her imagination was flailing. If it was Ben in the dark... she could find out if she charged through the undergrowth.

Yet what if he was waiting there, smiling? Waiting for her to come closer, to move further from the light and deeper into the anonymity of the trees. She'd be at his mercy and no-one would see if he hurt her. Or worse, know if he killed her. Was he that far gone?

Damn him.

Lisa backed into the daylight, keeping an eye on the shadows.

She climbed through the fence again then jogged for the car, glancing over her shoulder several times. Always the trees were still, empty. He hadn't been there. Just her imagination. No breathing, no smiling in the dark.

If she wanted answers there was another place to check.

The room beneath the stairs.

With one more glance at the distant smoke, she returned to the house. Dirt scraped against slate beneath her boots. The moment she reached the door, the feeling returned in a long, sick wave. The front door was still ajar. If something lurked down there it was something unnatural.

She went for her mobile but swore. It was at home, charging. She found the Drummond's phone and dialled Robert; best to leave Gerry out of it. No answer. She left a message and set the tyre iron down a moment. Then she shifted the furniture from in front of the door but stopped when a shiver rippled across her entire body – like oily hands over her skin.

The sensation lingered when she reached for the handle. Gritting her teeth, she pulled the door open. Steps led down to darkness. She flicked the light switch – nothing.

"Fine." Lisa dragged the table before the door, propping it open. The small amount of light it ensured was better than nothing, but she still went back to the car for her Maglite. The greasy, slick sensation swimming across her skin faded but it returned the moment she reached the stairs.

One hand carried the torch and the other gripped the iron.

The beam cleaved the dark as she descended, pausing at the bottom to wrinkle her nose. Something was 'off.' Like bad meat. She tried to slow her breathing as the torchlight passed over shelves stacked with tools and piles of boxes and plastic tubs, each marked in the handwriting of Ben's mother – the same graceful loops that Lisa had always seen on birthday and Christmas cards.

Jennifer, a kind woman. Nothing like her son.

If he'd hurt her...Lisa squeezed the iron again. What was she thinking? He'd been acting strange but shit, he wouldn't kill his own parents. Yet, the scratching in the room above, the blood in the sink – was it another roo attack? Misplaced vengeance? Hard to imagine a kangaroo managing the stairs.

The weight of the oil against her skin increased, as if she'd entered a pool that grew deeper with each step. Something blue flashed in the torchlight beyond a stack of boxes. The corner of a tarp? She pushed through the feeling, blinking against it when she reached the boxes – only to fall against them.

Piles of skin lay in the centre of the tarp.

Flecked red and pink, the folds sagged over one another. Some pieces were stretched, so thin as to appear translucent beneath the shaking beam of her torch. Other clumps were thick with hair and several pieces bore even edges, cuts, each a deep red. At the edge of the pile rested a large toenail and one patch of skin bore black marks – tattooed skin.

The outline of the Southern Cross.

A garbled sound was swallowed up by the dark basement and Lisa spun, raising the torch.

Alone. No-one. Nothing.

The sound had been a groan. "Oh God." She'd made the sound herself.

Lisa forced her body forward, checking the pile again, shining the beam on the tattoo. The five stars of the Southern Cross. Ben's tattoo, Ben's tattoo. She moved the torchlight higher – a bench with a sink stood beyond the pile. Resting atop lay a tin tray lined with surgical implements – a scalpel most prominent, its tip a deep red.

Ordered.

Neat, just like the pile and the tarp itself. Nothing an animal could achieve.

Human hands had done the bloody work.

Her breath came a little harder and the beam wavered as she shifted it along the bench. And stopped.

A huge skull sat atop a pile of moist earth. Longer than anything human, with deep grooves for eye sockets, it almost looked to have a beak – but it was no bird.

Kangaroo.

The bone had yellowed to a deep brown in places and cracks covered the surface, but the teeth remained. Despite the apparent decay, the thinness of some parts, the skull was whole.

Ancient.

And the greasy, sickening feeling of wrongness poured from it.

Malice washed over her as a light flashed in the eyes.

Something crashed above. She spun. Glass shattered and a shadow passed before the door – just a silhouette – but no shape she could fathom. Leaping for the stairs, Lisa cried out when the door was slammed as if by a great force. She climbed, taking them two at a time, to crash into the door. It didn't budge. Where was the handle? She beat against the surface with the iron. "Let me out," she cried.

No answer except a shuffling from beyond and more breaking glass.

She continued to beat on the door until her arms grew heavy – anything was better than being trapped with the skin, the skull and the weight of the oil. She'd dropped the torch – she'd been hammering the door in pitch black.

Lisa slumped against the wood and cast the iron aside. It clanged down to the concrete. Fumbling for the Maglite, her fingers wrapped around the shaft. Twisting the head, she shook the light and it blinked on.

Yet it made no difference.

Trapped.

Chapter 21.

"Lisa? Hello? Lisa, are you here?"

Robert's voice, muffled by the door. She stood and thumped on the grain. "In here," she called. Footsteps approached. "Beneath the stairs."

"I'm here," he said, voice nearly covered by the scrape of furniture. The door swung open and she blinked against the light, stumbling free. Robert took her arm and led her to a chair across from the plate of grass. "What happened? Are you all right?"

She nodded. "I think so. Thanks."

"Are you sure? You're covered in sweat," he said, crouching before her.

Lisa wiped her forehead. It was almost odd that her hand wasn't covered in thick oil – only salty sweat. She glanced at a silver clock on the wall. Lunchtime. "I was in there for a couple of hours I guess."

"I was in the back garden," he said. "I didn't get your message until just now."

"It's not your fault." She couldn't stop the shaking in her hands.

"Let me get you some water," he said, moving around the bench.

She straightened in the chair. "Not from there."

"Why not, it's –" He stopped, eyes widening. "What's going on?"

"Not in here." She started for the door. "We should talk outside."

By the Holden she took a moment to breathe in hot air, leaning against the warm driver's door. Anything was better than the basement. Lurking over the hills, the column of smoke had spread across a third of the sky. "Something's happened to Ben."

"Is he dead too?"

"I think so...it's like Fat – like James and Steven."

He looked away. "I heard about that. I'm sorry I didn't call you. I dropped around but you were with your dad and then I had an appointment with the specialist."

"It's fine. Really. Are you okay?"

"They're doing tests for diabetes. Maybe now we'll know why I crave all that juice, hey?" He waved a hand. "Don't worry about me though. If it's diabetes, it's diabetes. I'll work it out. Just tell me what's going on here."

"I found a lot of skin on a blue tarp down there. It was bloody, like it'd been removed on purpose."

His face paled. "Skin?"

"One patch had a tattoo of the southern cross, just like Ben."

"You should call Gerry."

"No – he'll have to tell McConnell."

"And he thinks you're responsible?"

She nodded, filling him in on the visit and the shadowy figure that locked her inside. "McConnell is running out of suspects."

He shook his head. "This is crazy."

"I know."

"Well, I heard Ronnie gossiping. Says that Karen told him about Lindgren."

"What about him?"

"His wounds were all made by an animal – so unless McConnell thinks you trained a kangaroo, I don't think he'll be charging you with anything."

"Yeah, well, we'll see."

He leaned beside her on the car. "What about Ben? Do you think he locked you in?"

"I don't know. I don't know...how much skin can a person cut off and survive?"

"How much was down there?"

"A lot."

"Sounds like someone did something to him." He paused, as if unsure of his next words. "I know this isn't right to say, but I don't think you should be too upset. He was no good, Lisa."

"I know," she said softly.

"But if someone did that to him – you have to ask, who's out there?"

She stared at the smoke building along the skyline. "Maybe it is Ben, somehow."

He frowned. "You think he removed his own skin?"

"Or just his tattoo, as a decoy – and the rest is from someone else."

"What? You mean his mum and dad?"

"Sounds stupid, doesn't it." She rubbed her eyes. It was all ridiculous. Hideous. And none of it made sense, no matter how she tried to explain it.

"We can find out. Or tell Gerry and they'll test the blood left on the skin. Or call them, do you have their number?"

"I don't know if I can go back in there," she said. "It turned my stomach."

"I'll go in, if you like," he said, pushing from the car.

She caught his arm. "No."

"I don't mind," he said.

She opened her mouth to tell him that something was wrong. The sense of it. The oily sensation, the ancient skull, the white kangaroo and the vision. But even Robert wouldn't believe that. "Let McConnell find it himself. He'll be back soon enough."

"If you say so."

"I just want to go home and have a shower. Try and forget about it for a while."

"All right, if you're sure. Give me a call if you need."

"I will."

She climbed into the car and drove around the owl statue before following Robert back into town. She tapped the steering wheel with both thumbs and leant her head against the glass of the driver's window at the lights. When she finally turned into Chambers Street and then her driveway, it couldn't have come a second sooner.

Inside, Lisa threw her clothes to the floorboards and leapt into the shower where she turned the hot water on hard and scrubbed herself, sighing as she did. There had never been any oil on her skin but the water blasted away the memory.

Didn't do the trick for the image of skin piled on a blue tarp.

Or the kangaroo skull.

Was it Ben? If it was, who'd do something that sick? Not Robert. He hadn't been too upset but still, not Robert. And not Gerry either – he might have been happy to rough Ben up, but he wasn't going to skin him. Dave? Not likely. No-one would. No sane person, anyway.

"Admit it, you're still the best suspect," she told the frosted glass.

Later, she forced down dry crackers and water before calling the hospital. Dad was undergoing more tests but he'd been awake since she left, which was something. Next, she tried Ben's parents as she paced the lounge. If Jennifer or Paul answered – or they didn't answer – which would be worse? But neither did and she didn't leave a message. They were probably travelling – not unusual for the Drummonds to spend a month in Europe. And she couldn't really tell them anything for certain anyway.

Instead, she slumped in the old creaking armchair and listened to updates about the fires – no progress toward Yarsdale – until she finally swore and stood.

Short of staking out the Drummond house, there was only one other way of finding answers – and even then, it was a gamble. But anything had to be better than hanging around waiting for something to happen. Or trying to go to work.

She had to see the white kangaroo again.

*

Even sitting square beneath the Wildlife Centre's ceiling fan, Sally fanned herself with an old baseball cap. "I guess we could do without it for a couple of hours."

"You can use the Holden in the meantime," she said.

She sighed – more from the heat than Lisa's request, it seemed. "I've got my car too, we'll be fine. I'll tell Colin when he gets back."

"Thanks, Sal." She accepted the keys. The vision of the ute being attacked flashed in her mind but she had an answer for her fears. Two people in the vision. One person collecting the keys now. "I'll be back by four."

"Don't stress."

"Thanks."

Sally folded her arms on the counter. "You okay? You know, with all the shit that's been going on?"

"I think so. It's like the animals have all gone crazy."

"I know. Saw something strange myself, you know."

"What was it?"

She tossed the hat onto the desk. "A line of foxes back on Stanberry Reserve. All dead, all in a row – as if they'd been following one another and simply died one at a time."

Her stomach twisted. What now? Ben? Something else? "That is strange," Lisa said. Outward, she kept her composure – or so she hoped. "Maybe we need to get someone to test the creeks."

Sally nodded. "Might be worth it."

"Well, I better get started." She headed out and jumped into the ute, adjusting the seat then heading for Pumps' farm. She tapped her thumb on the wheel as she drove. Stanberry Reserve ran behind Chambers Street – had the foxes been heading for her house?

Maybe the white roo could show her an answer for that too.

It was a long shot but it was all she had.

At least the ute would make things easier. Jennings Lane ran behind Pumps' farm and gave access to the dirt trails like the Dump Track near the shelter. Some of the lane was pretty rough but unlike her Holden, the ute had four-wheel drive. Once she left the highway, Lisa switched on the radio. More updates about the fire. No immediate danger to the area and no embers yet – but residents were being advised to continue to monitor news stations.

"Don't worry," she told the radio, ignoring the way her heart gave a flutter. The fire wasn't that close yet. But while it was sound advice – the announcers couldn't promise much more – radio signal could only go so deep into the bush. She'd have to rely on more than just official word.

More eucalyptus rose alongside the road, adding to the classic, muddy green seen in every Frederick McCubbin oil painting. In Jennings Lane, tendrils of bark peeled from the older trees. Not far into the lane she hopped out to unhook a shonky-looking gate. On the other side, once she'd closed the gate, she turned a switch inside the wheel hubs, engaging four-wheel drive.

She continued down the road, moving slowly around jagged potholes. A steep rise appeared and she picked up a little speed then put the foot down. Once over the crest, she paused to take a drink from her water bottle.

Trees thickened around the lane, growing closer, blocking more light. One had fallen across the road sometime in the past; the clean cut of a chainsaw had faded to grey where the trunk was shorn through. The day hadn't cooled; dopey flies bugged her at the window and she swatted at them, easing the ute along the dirt.

By the time she reached the dirt-bike trails, she'd tried two lesser paths branching from Jennings Lane to no avail, having to back out of some tight spots. Sweat was trickling between her shoulder blades. Branches grew across the lane. One slipped into her window, dumping a heap of wattle flowers into her lap.

"Damn it." She brushed at the clinging pollen and drove on, soon coming to a halt. There. The right one, finally. Entry to the Dump Track. Too narrow for the ute, but it wouldn't be too far to the shelter, hopefully. She cut the engine and found her torch, grabbed the water bottle and slipped the keys into her pocket before setting down the trail.

The same sandy, salt-and-pepper ground underfoot. The air tasted faintly of smoke – either that or she was imagining it. The bush was too dense to see much of the sky, but further up into the high country the fire would be raging. And somewhere up there the fire-fighters everyone depended on would be fighting it. Risking their lives.

"Stay safe," she murmured as she stepped over a twisted tree root.

She sipped from the water as she walked.

When she found the stand of trees growing up the sides of the shelter, half an hour had passed. In daylight, the red of the door was easier to spot but it was still concealed heavily by branches, even if some were bent from her last visit. She pushed through and tried the door.

It slid open with less resistance than before. The same stench hit her upon entering. She lifted the Maglite and this time daylight added its touch to the white kangaroo, though the interior remained dim, turning the fur grey.

Lisa knelt by her again. Nothing moved in the eye.

How did she even address the kangaroo? "Can you help me?"

No change.

"I need to find Ben. I need to know what's happening. Is he alive? Who locked me in the basement?" She rested a hand on the soft fur. "Can you show me?"

Still nothing.

"Please?"

The blood had dried to black in the sandy floor beneath her chest. The eye did not blink, no images flashed within. She was truly gone. Lisa's shoulders slumped. She'd come for nothing. Shouldn't have been surprised. 'Slim' barely described her chances. "Sorry to disturb your rest."

Lisa headed from the shelter. What now? She'd have to find Ben somehow.

She started back but stopped, cocking her head. Beneath the scent of distant smoke something else lurked. Just like the first time she visited. Something off, not unlike the smell in the shelter. Only worse. It grew as she walked. A dead wombat. Or another roo? She patted her shirt pocket. Her pouch would be close to empty – but even a few grains were worth sharing. She pushed through the branches, twigs cracking and the swish of heavy leaf-cover loud.

Beyond the screen stretched trampled ground, littered with bones and corpses – kangaroos. In heaps and pairs or lying alone, legs twisted, tails bloodied and worst of all, bones showing, flies buzzing.

Lisa cried out.

Something had been eating them.

The nearest animal had been stripped of flesh, gnaw marks on the thigh bone. Head and torso were still covered in fur. Some were even missing whole limbs. Torsos or heads.

No salt could remedy what lay before her.

She moved deeper with trembling steps – old bones peeked from the leaves everywhere she turned. She passed the skeletons of smaller animals; bilbies, wallabies and even the decomposing frame of a goanna. To her left was a wombat – a pair of koalas, their paws missing, to her right.

In the centre of the boneyard she stopped, tears stinging her eyes.

Scores of them.

Leaves rustled and she spun.

A kangaroo stood on the edge of the clearing. Too tall. Too broad – like the white kangaroo – only its fur was a deep red. Crimson, streaked with black clots and tangles. As if blood had seeped through the fur and stained it permanently. A growl rose from its throat but it didn't approach. Forepaws twitched.

She took a step back.

"What are you?" Lisa whispered.

The tail thumped once and it padded forward. Its breath was ragged. Lisa took another step. The great roo snarled until she stopped. She had nothing, no weapon but the torch. Yet when the blood-red kangaroo approached, when it neared her, she didn't run. She couldn't.

Its eyes were human.

Chapter 22.

The kangaroo's face glistened red. Rank breath passed over the jagged teeth where the beast towered above her. Its black nose had been sliced open at one point, healing poorly. Even the fur was knotted with dried blood. But it was the eyes that caught her. Human, somehow they were human. Larger than natural, the eyes were spread across the dark face, but undeniably those of a man; whites showing. Not the normal brown of a roo.

"Ben?"

The kangaroo snorted, shoulders trembling.

"Are you in there?"

Its head snapped forward. She threw her arm up and gnashing teeth clamped down – not hard enough to break skin. Saliva pooled on her forearm as the great jaws locked her arm between gaps in the teeth. She strained against it but the kangaroo held tight. The stench of death washed over her.

The eyes had rolled back to brown.

She screamed. Its head jerked, tossing her to the ground where something sharp bit into her thigh. Lisa scrambled back, hands fumbling over fur and bone. The red kangaroo leapt after her, ground vibrating when it landed. The tail whipped around and crashed beside her. Bone fragments flew, stinging her cheek, and warm blood trickled down her jaw.

The kangaroo's eyes rolled again.

It turned to bound away, and she scrambled to her feet. Her shoulders stiffened when she caught a glimpse of five stars – the Southern Cross – pink against the red fur.

And then the roo was gone, crashing through branches.

Lisa moaned. Ben was the creature. Ben was the figure in the vision – the man with the rifle who'd fallen down to undergo a transformation into a blood-red kangaroo. Ben was the one who'd shed skin in the basement of his own home. The blood stains on his jeans, the blood in the sink, the droppings, the carpet...the skull.

Run. Just run. Get out of the boneyard.

Back to town; find help.

Out of the graveyard and her feet pounded dirt as she charged back toward Jennings Lane. She ran until her lungs seared and her throat rasped, finally stumbling up to the ute. The afternoon sun had tinted it orange and she let out a strangled cry when she saw it, relief turning her limbs to jelly.

Beautiful – it could take her away.

She fumbled for her keys, wincing when she twisted – her jeans were unbroken but the flesh of her thigh was tender. She climbed into the driver's seat and when she turned to reverse out of the lane, she winced again. In the first run-off she made a three-point turn, checking the mirrors.

No sign of the red roo.

At least now, facing the direction she was travelling, she could pick up speed. She tried to slow her breathing, to focus on the turns and overhanging branches.

Instead, she gripped the wheel hard enough for the leather to squeak.

How had it happened? Ben was gone. He was the bloody kangaroo now, keeper of an animal graveyard. It wasn't possible. It couldn't be. Could it?

But why not?

The white kangaroo was real.

On her forearm, saliva covered her skin, hairs sticking together.

The red kangaroo was real too.

And it saved her. Or Ben did.

When the eyes rolled from white, that had to be whatever dark force possessed him, right? The red giant had attacked and Ben had held it off. Didn't he? She groaned as she accelerated out of a bend. Would it always be so? Or would the kangaroo – the thing of death – would it consume him?

If it hadn't done so already.

Or she was fooling herself? A shiver ran across her shoulders. Since when had Ben wanted to protect her? Maybe he'd given himself up willingly; he'd been a hate-filled man before. He'd been responsible for so much pain and death, and he'd killed the white kangaroo. But why? As a claim to fame? Perhaps he'd found out what Pumps was up to and tried to steal his thunder.

Maybe it was all the red kangaroo. Maybe the red kangaroo had existed before Ben, maybe it took his soul?

Maybe that explained the skull in the basement.

Shit, was it really even him? How could a man even become that...that thing? Maybe she was insane.

"Enough," she shouted. Too many questions and no real answers.

She'd never know how it happened. Whatever 'it' was.

Just head back to town. Get away.

No-one was in at the Wildlife Centre so she swapped the ute for her Holden and headed home. This time her clothes went into the bin and her shower was quick. She grabbed her phone and called Gerry.

"Lisa? Are you okay?"

"No, I just wanted to ask. Did you or McConnell find Ben yet?"

"Not yet."

"Damn it." She knew why.

"I'm just at the pub, if you want me to –"

"Actually, I could use something to eat. I'll be there soon." Perfect – somewhere with hot food and lots of people. Somewhere normal.

At the pub, she paused in the doorway, letting the conversation and clink of cutlery wash over her. Normal. Beautifully normal. Bruce waved from behind the bar, halfway through pulling a drink. She moved in, nodding to the regulars, who didn't appear all that pleased to see her; thanks to the rumour mill, she supposed. She found Gerry and sat beside him at the end of the row.

"Are you all right? Has Ben done something?" He was still in uniform and a half-finished bowl of pasta rested before him. Carbonara – the smell of bacon and creamy sauce.

"No, I'm just getting tired of waiting..." She hesitated.

Don't be stupid. He wouldn't believe her. Who would? "I'm on edge, all the time."

He hesitated slightly then put an arm around her shoulders. "I understand, but we'll find him. He can't hide forever and Lidelson's not that big. Why don't you get something to eat?"

She closed her eyes and leant against him for just a moment. "Good idea."

"Great, I'll keep you company if you like?" His phone interrupted before she could answer. He gave an apologetic smile as he took the call. "Hansen."

The voice on the other end was muffled but a sense of urgency slipped through.

"I'm on my way." He hung up.

"Trouble?" Was it Ben?

"I have to go, I'm sorry. I'll drop by tomorrow, all right?" And then he was gone.

Bruce appeared, a tea-towel slung over his shoulder. "You look knackered."

"I am." She rubbed at her eyes. "I need a drink and I could use a parma too," she said.

"Draught?"

"Better make it a light beer," she said.

"Righto." He soon returned with a beer, setting it down. "I'll get young Matt working on your tea too."

"Thanks, Bruce." She took a long drink. Bitter. Fitting, too. "You look tired yourself," she said.

He shrugged. "I've been checking the gutters and roof, you know? Fire season after all and you don't wanna cut corners there. Life and death, right?" He collected a few empty glasses. "Gotta be ready. I went and got some window shields too, just in case."

"Good idea," she said, though she couldn't put much conviction into her response. He gave her a smile and moved off to help one of his other customers.

She spun one of the thin coasters while she waited, staring at the framed photos behind the bar. Rally cars, a dusty B-Double and a pin-up shot – only Bruce had drawn a moustache and beard on the model; he liked to tell everyone it was his ex-wife.

The drone of conversation and the clack of pool balls filled her ears as the early evening wore on. When Matthew appeared he set a steaming plate down. Chips and salad piled high around a slab of chicken parmigiana. Her mouth actually watered – spraying a fine haze of droplets onto the counter.

"Hungry, eh?" Matthew chuckled.

She wiped at the counter and took the knife and fork, able to manage a smile. "Yeah. Thanks, Matt."

"Hey, you right?" He leant on the counter.

If only. "Just exhausted. Actually, do you know anyone who knows much about kangaroo myths?"

"Like Dreamtime stories?"

"I guess so."

"Not really. Why don't you try the primary school or the library? They'll know someone." He slapped the counter as he straightened with a grin. "Or look it up online, stupid."

"Of course." She laughed. He returned to the kitchen and she got stuck into the food.

When she was done, she leant against the wall where it met the bar. What a difference a full stomach made. And the company of other people. Even leaning kept pressure off her thigh, which still ached. Matthew was right; she could start with the internet. Maybe there'd be something about kangaroos gone feral. Maybe there was a Dreamtime story about them. There *was* at least one she sort of recalled from school. How the Kangaroo Got his Tail? But that probably wouldn't help much.

On the way out she tried to pay but Bruce raised his hands. "My treat, Lisa. Go home and rest."

"Thanks, Bruce. I owe you."

"No way. Just do as I say now, all right? Get an early night."

"I will."

Back home she locked up – yet the single glazed glass and bolt on the front door didn't seem like enough. Could it really stand up to the red kangaroo – or Ben – or whatever it was?

She switched the radio on. High winds expected overnight. And worse, a Northerly, which could easily drive the fire down toward Lidelson. Or Yarsdale – and Dad. She turned the radio down to a murmur and opened her laptop, a mug of coffee beside her. Too hot for coffee but she needed the caffeine.

The internet revealed no traditional myths about giant white or red kangaroos, nor cannibalistic, murderous kangaroo-gods either. No transformations and nor, for that matter, undead wildlife intent on vengeance. Had the red kangaroo sent the corpses after Fathead and Steve? As retribution? And now had it taken Ben too. Saving the ultimate punishment for the man who led them.

Would it stop? Would Ben be able to stop it, if there was anything of him left within, as it seemed? She shivered. Maybe the white kangaroo was the only thing that could stop the beast.

Tomorrow would mean more research.

Or maybe she needed to find a gun and go hunting. It's what Dad would have suggested, but she hadn't touched a gun in years.

Could Robert help? No. He wouldn't believe her any more than Gerry would.

Which meant no-one was going to help her. Not willingly at least. She might be able to trick Robert, or Gerry for that matter, into hunting down a 'feral roo' with her but risking their lives wasn't right. She had to take control of her life again. It'd taken too long to get it back the first time Ben had taken everything away – he wasn't going to do it again.

Even as a blood-covered kangaroo.

She had to act. Alone. Lisa reached for the mug, wrapping her hands around it and tapping her foot slowly beneath the table. If she could hunt it, if she could shoot it, would that be enough? Would it even die? The roo that killed Steve was a corpse. Same with the snake.

Could she shoot it down and cut it to pieces? She needed a big gun, like Pumps' Remington. It took .308 rounds, the largest calibre a civilian was going to get. And once she had the gun, she needed to keep out of sight. If McConnell or even Gerry saw her practising with a rifle they'd try and stop her. McConnell might even decide to lock her up. Or worse, one of them could try and help her.

And before all of that, she had to see Dad.

Just in case.

Chapter 23.

Lisa cancelled her jobs for the day and paced through a news broadcast. She'd set two alarms – one for midnight and another for three in the morning – to check the ABC radio. Bleary-eyed and limping, each time the report confirmed the fire was not yet threatening Lidelson or Yarsdale – Dad was safe for the time being.

And once again the newsreader gave them the all clear.

Overnight, however, the wind had driven the firewall down toward small high country towns and isolated homes – all of which had been evacuated, but a second fire had taken hold to the east. The announcer's voice was weary. "This new fire is smaller than the alpine complex but if the wind is unkind, the two may join. It's not known at this stage if the fire was deliberately lit."

Lisa slapped the bench top. Pieces of shit. If someone started it on purpose...

She exhaled. Focus. She had to stop Ben. Or the red kangaroo, whatever he'd become. Something had killed

Clint Healy, or forced a kangaroo to do so. Something had given Pumps the fright of his life – and maybe that was the white roo returning, maybe it was Ben. And it felt right if the kangaroo had made sure James and Steven died too.

And now it had to die.

If it was even possible, then killing it would be the mercy she showed Ben. And maybe he didn't truly deserve her mercy, but then, no-one deserved whatever was happening to him. Or perhaps, whatever he'd done to himself. Somehow. Damn fool.

Even after everything he'd done, for some reason it seemed he'd saved her in the boneyard. She hoped. Or perhaps it was just a warning.

Whatever had happened, she would put a stop to it.

She had to kill Ben. Or whatever he'd become.

But before all that she had to see Dad.

She'd barely left Chambers Street before the orange warning light blinked on – petrol running low. She pulled into Johnno's – a two-pump station – and filled the Holden. The attendant watched from the window, the rest of the brick building painted a peeling white. Still the same – it hadn't been done up since before her week of work experience back in high school. Not that they'd remember her; Johnno had long since moved on.

Inside the station she grabbed a Turkish Delight, paid up and headed for the car, stopping when a police cruiser pulled in behind her.

Gerry climbed out and waved. "Hi."

Good. It wasn't McConnell. "Hi. Any news?"

He rubbed his jaw – unshaven, which was unusual for him. He was obviously stressed too. "There's been another murder. That's where I had to go last night. Someone from out of town; poor bastards were just passing through. The next truck stop along from where you found Clint. Slashed up pretty bad. Looks like claw marks."

Her heart skipped a beat. "What?"

"I know. We've had a missing person report come in too."

Lisa sagged against the car. How much worse was it going to get? All the killings. Were they just random? Or was it retribution? "Couple of high school kids haven't been seen for two days."

"Maybe they went on a road trip or something."

"I haven't ruled that out." He glanced at the Holden. "Heading to the hospital?"

"Yeah. I haven't seen him for a day or so."

"Hope he's doing better," Gerry said.

"Me too." She paused. Gerry would help if she asked. At the least, he'd be willing to keep an eye on her, but only if she sold it like hunting a real kangaroo – not a huge, red beast or a vengeful bush-God.

But that wasn't fair. She'd be putting him in danger and he'd looked out for her since Ben revealed his true colours; Gerry didn't deserve that.

He moved closer, concern clear on his face. "You all right?"

She nodded. "Still tired I guess."

"McConnell?"

"Everything." She shrugged. "He thinks I'm involved, doesn't he?"

"You know I shouldn't talk about that with you."

"I know."

He grinned. "Let's just say he's not one to make assumptions and the autopsies seem to point to animal attacks. We're all pretty confused actually."

"Do you think it's animals, like the kangaroo I saw?"

"I do. And that's what the evidence suggests. But I gotta say, must be one hell of a mean roo."

"Maybe it's time someone tried to track it. It could be sick – that might be making it crazy."

"Not a bad idea. But that's for someone higher up the food chain than me to decide." He paused, as if wanting to say more. "Drive safe." He returned to the cruiser.

Lisa got back on the road. The morning was not yet fully underway when she reached Yarsdale Hospital where it sat on the hill, looking down across the rows of tiled rooves interspersed with corrugated iron. Once again, she waited at the nurse's station, with its blinking phones and cluttered notice boards, for a nurse to take her in to see Dad.

"How is he today?" she asked.

The woman clipped a pen to a board and put it aside. Her expression was not encouraging. "Dr Bagnato had to sedate him. He became very agitated when he couldn't understand why he was in hospital. He demanded to see Annie."

Her shoulders slumped. "Is he lucid?"

"For the most part but he hasn't been talkative," she said, her tone kind. "When we bring him some lunch he might perk up a bit."

"Do you know why he collapsed?"

"It's likely related to his condition," she said. "You can find him just down there. Number three."

"Thanks." Lisa walked down the hall and into room three, where she pulled back the curtain around Dad's bed.

He blinked up at her from the sheets. "Yes?" His eyes showed no recognition.

Lisa forced a smile. "It's Lisa. How are you feeling?"

"Well enough I suppose." He frowned at her. "Have we met?"

Oh God, Dad. Why aren't you here? "I'm...I've visited before," she said. No point upsetting him. At least he didn't look to be in pain.

He waved to the chair. "Well, you look friendly enough. Have a seat."

She did. "Ah...so, how are you?"

He grinned. "You need some practice at this. Community service or volunteer?"

"Volunteer."

"Well, why don't you ask me something you don't already know? Should be obvious I'm not doing too well," he said, but he was still smiling.

"Good idea, yeah. Okay...so, what would you be doing now? If you were home, instead of here?"

"That's better." He tapped his thumb on the steel rail of the bed, a small bandaid on the back of his hand. "I'd be painting, I guess. Feels like I haven't done it in a while and I miss it."

'A while' was fifteen years. Since Mum died.

"I can ask if they have anything here?"

"Can't hurt."

"So, what would you paint?" He used to do Impressionist landscapes and scenes of the town. Maybe kids playing in a dam or the old post office – before they replaced it when she was a kid. She still had some of his oils, like the butterfly and caterpillar. There had been others, but he'd hidden them away somewhere after Mum...

"Rose garden. Or a Labrador – always wanted one."

"Why didn't you?" But she knew the answer – Mum had been allergic.

"Can't remember." He fell silent.

Lisa glanced away, fighting tears. He wasn't going to remember. Maybe it was time to leave. There was every chance she wouldn't even find the red kangaroo and she'd be back to see him again; that the fire wouldn't reach Lidelson or Yarsdale. That the medication would start to work and he'd remember for a little longer.

But just in case...She stood. "I'll check for those paints then."

"That'd be good," he said.

She hesitated. "Would you mind if I gave you a kiss on the cheek?"

"A pretty girl like you? Of course not."

She laughed, leant in and kissed his cheek, closing her eyes as tears threatened again. At least he was smiling. When she pulled back she blinked, mumbled a goodbye and nearly dashed from the room.

He called after her but she didn't slow.

After all, he probably wouldn't remember.

Chapter 24.

Pumps' farm was quiet beneath the noon sun, which bore down on the tin roof from behind a haze of smoke, like a furious orange ball. Police tape surrounded the tractor, torn at one end, blue and white checks fluttering in the hot breeze. The taste of ash had grown heavy on the air overnight.

The house was closed up – maybe some relative had come to check over his belongings – but she went around to the back door and lifted the bucket beside the outdoor tap. Earwigs twisted and scurried away. She flicked one from the silver key and fitted it to the door. She paused. "Sorry, Pumps. Hope you understand."

She turned the key.

No radio this time. Work clothes soaked in a concrete sink in the laundry and a Western lay open on an armchair in the sunroom opposite. At the end of the passage she turned into the lounge where the sleek, black Remington hung over the mantle.

Lisa hesitated.

Long time since she'd held a gun. Not since Granddad's farm. He'd had one of his big hands on her shoulder, his rasping voice low as he explained how to hold the weapon, where to rest the butt; how to be gentle with the trigger.

Too bad, Lisa. Take it, do what has to be done.

She lifted it down, heavier than she'd expected, and pulled the bolt free. A .308 round lay within; the magazine held four at a time, and she'd need more. She checked the bottom drawer in the kitchen, atop the old fridge and a cabinet in the bedroom before opening the cupboard, where she reached up to the top shelf, feeling around until she gripped a box. Pulling it down, she gave a nod. Winchester .308. The bullets rattled as she hurried back outside, slinging the rifle over her shoulder and locking up again.

Then it was back onto the road – first stop, the Drummond's place.

Or at least, first place she'd drive by. If Detective McConnell was there, then she'd keep going. Maybe head back out to Jennings Lane or the truck stops on Swallow's Road. No way to know where Ben would be, but she had to try them all.

No silver sedan at the Drummond's – and no sign of Ben, his parents or any kangaroo when she climbed out of the car. Lisa lifted the rifle, resting it across her forearm as she walked toward the house. She stopped. Going back inside... stupid. The red roo wouldn't be in there – it'd be out in the bush, waiting for night. And the house still had the pile of skin and the skull with its bad vibes in the basement. Bad vibes – that was an understatement.

His parents had better be on holiday; if he'd done something to them...

She headed for the trees, the last place she'd seen the dark figure.

When she neared the fence a magpie took flight. She swung the barrel around but didn't fire. Just a bird, Lisa. She took a shuddering breath. Just a bird. She put a foot on the wire but before she could slip through, her mobile interrupted. McConnell. She slung the rifle back and answered.

"Detective McConnell. Am I in hot water again?"

"This isn't a time for jokes, Miss Thomas."

"I know. Is your mum safe?"

"For now." He paused. "And your father?"

"About the same." She started back toward her car; Ben wasn't here. There was no sense of being watched, no malice in the air. Was the boneyard the place then?

"I'd like you to come in to the station for further questioning, seeing as you're not presently at home."

"Why?"

"Because in addition to that tyre iron you were carrying around yesterday – we found a pile of what appears to be human skin in the Drummond's basement."

Damn it. Idiot – of course, she'd left it behind. But the bloody kangaroo came first. Unless...had McConnell seen the skull too? It was linked to Ben, maybe he needed it? Would he go after it, if the detective had taken it? "Ah, was there anything else down there?"

"Such as?"

"A kangaroo skull?"

"No. Why?"

Good. Maybe McConnell would be safe. "Ben used to collect them, maybe he came back for it."

"Miss Thomas, I'm not sure what that has to do with anything but I think it'd be best if you came in."

"I'll come down later."

"Now would be better."

"Gerry's looking for me, isn't he?"

"Karen actually."

She came to a halt at her car. "Well, there's something I have to do first."

"And what would that be exactly?"

"I have to shoot a feral roo." She hung up and put the rifle in the back, before climbing into the Holden. Time to pick up the speed. Stupid, giving McConnell a dramatic line. They'd check for her in some obvious places now. Like Swallow's Road – but as far as she knew they were unaware of the boneyard. Though if she had to lie in wait for days, they'd have to hone in eventually, wouldn't they?

She stomped on the pedal and roared out of the Drummond's and eventually back onto the main road, where she turned toward Swallow's. Once she'd put in some distance from the property, she pulled into a truck stop – not the one where Clint had died.

This time she kept the rifle in the backseat. No need to alarm passers-by, especially with the traffic. Holiday makers for the most part, their four-wheel drives and family car roof-racks laden with tents and kayaks – all charging back toward safer ground. The bleak yellow tint to everything was bad enough but the smoke in the air was growing heavier too. It clung to the sky like a scuffed blanket.

It was the worst time to head out to hunt a giant kangaroo in the bush. If the threat of a bushfire wasn't enough there was McConnell – but no-one else was going to do it. She stalked into the trees. Lisa closed her eyes but there was nothing. No sense of malice, just the hum of traffic.

Back to the car.

Only the boneyard left. She needed four-wheel drive for Jennings Lane; the Holden wasn't up to it. Would Karen or McConnell be waiting at the Wildlife Centre if she tried? It wasn't like she could just go hire a four-wheel drive. And Dad hadn't driven for years – but maybe, if she called Robert and asked him to meet on the turn? Sent him home right after.

He'd resist but if she insisted, Robert would have to listen.

*

When Robert arrived, driving the wildlife ute, she snapped the radio off. Damn it – she'd asked him to bring his own Land Cruiser. The vision of something dark hurtling into the ute flashed before her mind's eye. Had the white kangaroo been trying to show her the future, or only a possibility? It didn't matter. Robert would be taking the Holden home and that was that.

Only one person in the ute so no way for the vision to come true.

"What's wrong?" he asked. "And why did you want to meet here?"

"I can't get very far into the lane without something like the ute."

"I know that, but why? What's up there?" He handed her the keys.

"Thank you." She started moving her gear to the ute. Backpack, water, blanket – not that she'd need it in the heat.

"I'm going to kill the kangaroo that's causing all this trouble."

"You're hunting?" His expression was one of shock. "And how do you know it's a feral roo?"

"I saw it the other day and it's big." She lifted the rifle. "I want to be prepared."

"Woah, wait a minute. You hate killing."

"This is mercy. And I don't want anyone else to die. You heard about the tourist and the two kids?"

"Yeah. McConnell came to interview me about it."

"He ask about Ben?"

"Yeah, but I was at the shop with Kelli. Why?"

"Because McConnell thinks he can prove I'm responsible for the deaths and Ben's disappearance."

"Shit."

"Well, it doesn't matter. If I can stop the kangaroo everything will work out."

"Hey." He caught her arm. "It might not. If McConnell believes you're behind everything... This is getting serious, Lisa."

She smiled. "But you don't?"

"No way."

"Thanks." Her smile faded. If she asked, he'd stay...but that wouldn't be fair. Why risk two lives?

"Is something else going on?" he asked.

"No. Just this roo. I think it's bigger than normal. I think it killed Clint and somehow it's behind the other deaths."

"That doesn't make sense."

"Animals can cooperate. They'll protect each other, protect their young. You know that."

"They don't organise revenge killings."

"I think this one does."

He narrowed his eyes. "You're serious."

"Look, it doesn't matter what I think, does it? There's a large, crazed animal out there that's killing innocent people. It's probably sick, hurt and confused. Someone needs to put it to rest."

"So is it organised or confused, Lisa?"

"Please just take my car, Robert. If I'm not back tomorrow afternoon, come and find me, all right?" She held out her keys.

He took them. "I'm sorry. At least let me give you a hand. I've got the .22 in the back."

She glanced into the trees. There was another way. She could show him the white roo and then he'd see the sheer size and believe her about a predator. Only, it was still a risk. Even if two guns were probably better than one.

And there was still the vision.

"No. It's fine. I probably won't even find anything and I'll be back before lunch tomorrow."

"Bullshit, you're worried."

Lisa folded her arms. She'd been wrong about him; he wasn't going to just let her go. And if she didn't get a move on, Karen or McConnell or even Gerry would find her. She sighed. Damn. So long as she stayed away from clearings like the one in the vision. That'd be enough, wouldn't it? "Get in."

He ran around to the passenger side and Lisa took the driver's seat. She bypassed the Holden, which she'd pulled some of the way into undergrowth – not much of a hiding place – and started up Jennings Lane. This time Robert handled the crooked gate and before long she'd crested the hill again, also managing to avoid the wattle growing over the road, enough that she didn't fill the cab with pollen at least. It still scratched the door.

When she stopped at the fork to the Dump Track she glanced at Robert. "I want to check the radio, then we'll go if you're ready?"

"Good idea."

She turned the volume up. "...the wind is expected to change again around early evening and residents south of Pulla should Watch and Act, especially for ember-attacks. Districts around Yarsdale should expect to have their threat-level upgraded at short notice."

"Maybe this isn't such a good idea," Robert said.

"We're not in danger just yet." She clenched her fist. Who was she trying to convince with that line?

"Then we should come back and check regularly."

She nodded, collected the Remington and her pack while Robert pulled the .22 from the lockbox in the back. She led the way along the trail. The trees were quiet and the smoke cover had grown while they drove, it was almost enough to sting her eyes, even beneath the canopy.

"How far?" Robert asked. He carried the .22 without a strap.

"Not too far. There's an old depot nearby. It's close to something that looks like a hunting ground. And there's something I need to show you."

"What?"

"It's easier to show you."

"All right."

When they arrived, she wrinkled her nose. In the heat, the smell of the boneyard was strong.

"What reeks?" Robert asked.

"Let me show you something inside first." She dragged the door open, letting light in, and another wave of dying flesh hit. She coughed, then headed inside, flicking a torch on, this one smaller, seeing as she'd dropped the Maglite somewhere. In the open space, she stood aside, directing the torch to the white fur of the great kangaroo.

"Is that..." Robert bent slowly.

"She's real. I think Ben shot her."

He turned back to her, one cheek lit by her torch, the other in shadow. His eyes were wide. "But no roo can grow this big."

"That's what I thought at first."

Robert straightened, pacing out the length of the roo. He scratched his head. "How can no-one have seen something like her before?"

"There's some pretty remote places north of here."

"It's amazing."

"Well, the red one isn't."

"Red?"

"The other one is red. It's just as big but it's feral, Robert. Aggressive." She held his gaze. "Do you still want to help me?"

"I do." He looked to the white roo. "Maybe we should have brought bigger guns."

"There's two of us; it'll have to be enough."

"What now then?"

"We should find a good spot nearby." She led him back outside and through the trees to the boneyard, where she gave him a moment to take in the death. He'd had two shocks, best to let him process some of it.

He was rubbing a thumb across the grain of the rifle butt.

"This is all from one kangaroo?"

"I think so. It didn't like me being here."

"I don't like being here either," he said. He hefted the gun, gaze roving the grey messmate and paler gum trees. "Keep a line of sight on each other, right?"

"Right. Circle and meet on the other side."

He nodded.

She slipped into the trees, moving away from Robert. The thin trails meandered around the yard. None showed recent signs of use until she reached the point where the red kangaroo fled after the attack. Tiny branches struggling to grow from the trunks of nearby trees had been crushed and deep gouges lay in the earth. Just how big were the claws?

There was a trail nearby that led deeper into the bush – away from the Dump Track. Recent droppings, twisted and streaked with black blood, rested a little way down the trail. She turned back, meeting Robert nearby.

"I've found something. I think it's worth staking out." She showed him the path and the pile of droppings.

"All right. Let's watch this point then."

She nodded. "Get into the trees across from me. This trail can be the point of a triangle. Let him move into the clearing."

"Let's hope he doesn't wait too long." He frowned up at the haze between the trees. "That fire could charge at any time."

"We'll check the radio in a little while."

He moved back along the edge of the boneyard. Lisa returned to a spot opposite Robert, crouching between the trees, a broad messmate at her back. If nothing else, the smoke masked the scent of rotting flesh.

But Robert was right. Getting caught out here with a fire was suicide.

Yet Ben – the bloody kangaroo – had to be stopped and she'd only have one chance. If she failed here he'd avoid the boneyard from then on – animal or human cunning, either way, he'd know.

But he obviously wouldn't stop killing either.

No choice but to make sure.

The day wore on as she listened for clues to the kangaroo's return. Smoke thickened. A wind rose, even between the trees it tugged at her shirt. The taste of ash came with it. Sweat pooled in the small of her back and stung her eyes. She shifted position often, wiped at her brow and sipped from her water.

At one point she signalled for Robert to check on the radio. When he returned his face was set in a frown as he crouched near her. "They say the wind has already changed. We could have embers here any time. I think we should leave."

"Not yet," she said. "If there's a chance I want to take it."

"You won't get a chance if you're burnt to a crisp."

"Just a little longer."

He hesitated. "Fine. But the moment something changes we're leaving."

"Thank you."

He headed back to his side of the boneyard. She watched him settle into position then turned back to the mouth of the trail. Hurry up, Ben.

Time dragged. She stood, moving slowly, resting the rifle against the bark to stretch. She rolled her shoulders and heaved a sigh. Her throat was scratchy. Maybe it was time to leave after all. Still no embers; but by then it would have been too late.

Crashing leaves and branches broke the hush. She snatched the gun and dropped into a crouch, lifting the butt to her shoulder. She looked along the barrel but didn't put her eye to the scope yet – instead she checked on Robert.

He'd ducked out of sight. "Hope you're a good shot, Robert," she whispered.

She'd never seen him shoot at any distance.

Lisa exhaled slowly – she had to breathe. Her grandfather's scratchy voice echoed in her mind, calm, measured. *Don't tense up. Squeeze the trigger, try not to pull it. Keep the butt off the collar, use your dominant eye. Keep the damn barrel steady.*

All the right advice but she was still holding her breath. Her lungs were straining.

The crashing drew nearer.

She exhaled through her nose. Sweat trickled – everywhere it seemed. She flexed her grip. Grime lay beneath her nails. *Come on, Ben. Closer.* The hint of a shadow loomed across the clearing, hidden by the haze. It was him; had to be.

An ache grew in her shoulder and she swallowed.

"Come on."

And then the bloody kangaroo burst into the clearing.

Chapter 25.

The roo slowed, huge feet scattering bones and its tail set for balance. It stood, sniffing the air, ears twitching. With the smoke growing thicker and the fire-front nearing, the kangaroo wouldn't stay put long.

And hopefully it wouldn't be able to smell them.

Lisa swung the rifle around and steadied herself. Her grip on the rifle's forestock was sharp – her fingers were turning white and the butt was digging in. She exhaled and put her finger on the trigger.

Hesitated.

Could she really shoot an animal? Even knowing what it was? Was the red, corpse-like creature even an animal?

A shot cracked the air.

The kangaroo flinched, then wheeled on Robert's position and started forward, a growl crossing the clearing. Another shot from Robert and the roo barely faltered.

"Shit." Lisa adjusted for the roo's back and fired.

The recoil vibrated through her shoulder and a ringing

exploded in her ears but the kangaroo stumbled this time. It turned back toward her and Lisa drew the bolt between thumb and forefinger, snapping the chamber closed and aiming for the chest.

She pulled the trigger.

A cloud of red exploded before the roo. It fell to the side, stumbling along the ground but not collapsing. Instead, it scrambled upright, flinging bones in its wake. Lisa ducked the debris and snapped back up, rifle raised.

The red was heading for the treeline.

She worked the bolt and fired again. Missed – she'd rushed it. The kangaroo continued through the echo of shots from Robert. Lisa dashed into the clearing and steadied herself, raising the gun to fire again but stayed her finger – only the dark hint of its shape disappeared into the trees.

She needed a better shot. And with only one round left and the rest of the ammo in her bag, if she turned back to get it she'd lose the roo.

Lisa charged toward the smoke-choked trees. Something caught her shoulder.

Robert. His eyes were wide and he was breathing fast. "Lisa, no." He pointed at the smoke. "It's enough, we have to leave."

The wind had risen and smoke was swirling but as yet no flames were visible. "I have to be sure."

"We both had hits. Did you see? Some of the shots made bigger holes than normal, he'll bleed out."

She lowered the barrel. "You don't know that."

"I know we'll die out here if we don't leave. Look." He pointed through the trees. The sky was darkening. The fire was getting too close. Chasing the beast was suicide.

"Shit."

"Swear about it when we're safe." He pulled her toward the Dump Track. She glanced over her shoulder as they hit the dirt but the roo was gone. Ben was gone. If nothing else, smoke inhalation would finish him should the wounds fail. She tripped on a root that had clawed its way into the path but Robert caught her.

By the time the ute loomed from the haze, she was hacking, running stooped over. Had they left it too late? Robert tossed the .22 in the back and tore at the driver's door. Lisa slid across the bonnet and leapt into the passenger side. She slammed the door, resting the rifle between her knees, muzzle scraping the roof.

"Come on," Robert shouted. The ute responded with a roar, bringing the static of the radio with it. He flicked the lights on as he backed into a three point turn, working the pedals hard as smoke swirled around the windscreen. Trees twenty metres away were shrouded by pale smoke. Anything further away was lost, mere dark suggestions. Falling leaves flashed in the headlights, disappearing as quickly as they appeared.

Robert muttered as he drove, taking corners with sharp jerks of the wheel as he pushed the limits of a safe speed. He slowed at the steep slope.

"Will we make it?" Lisa asked. She glanced through the smudges on the back window. Was that a red glow back beyond the trees? Or just the eerie light of a smothered sun?

"I think so," he said, rolling down the hill.

"What if the road's cut?"

"Fire's still north of us."

The smoke eased when Jennings Lane exited onto the

highway, where Robert slammed the brakes on. Lisa was whipped forward, giving a shout when the seat belt dug into her shoulder. A log truck screamed down the hill, chains on the load clanging against the bunks. Robert clenched the wheel. "That was close."

"Keep going."

"What about your car?"

"Damn it." It was still hidden near the – something dark loomed at the edge of her vision. She spun in her seat. The dark shape slammed into the ute, rocking the one-tonne vehicle. Lisa flinched with a cry. The bloodied kangaroo! It wheeled then leant back on its tail, delivering a massive kick with both powerful hind legs. Glass shattered and she whipped her head to the side as fragments filled the cab.

"Drive!"

Robert slammed the pedal to the floor and the vehicle lurched onto the asphalt. She leant out the empty window, dragging hair from her eyes. The kangaroo bounded after them. Blood slipped from various wounds, a huge chunk of flesh missing from the chest. It was keeping pace with the ute. Easily over sixty kilometres an hour – impossible.

"Faster."

"Are you okay?"

The ute picked up speed, engine roaring, and the kangaroo began to recede into the smoke that covered the road, covered the bush. Yet it didn't stop hopping after them. A regular kangaroo wouldn't have been able to manage even forty kilometres over a short distance, let alone stay within sight for such a long time.

Robert skidded around a sharp bend and she pulled back. In the mirror, the dark kangaroo was gone. Only the smouldering red sky flashing between trees.

"Lisa?" He wheezed, fumbling with a water bottle he'd found from somewhere. "Is it there?"

"No. Did you see it?"

"It kept up with us for a little while." He handed her the bottle.

She drank; warm water but still a blessing. "I know."

Robert's grip on the wheel turned his knuckles white. "How can it be real?"

"I don't know. It doesn't matter, does it?"

He didn't say anything. Lisa lay back in the seat, gripping the rifle. Her throat burned, even her nose was raw. How many bullets had the roo taken and still it chased them. Was Ben driving it on? It couldn't be just his rage anymore – there had to be something else, the kangaroo itself. After all, he'd spared her – hadn't he? Unless it was the kangaroo who tried to stop Ben. Were the two now one and the same?

The outskirts of Lidelson were just as smoke-smothered as the road itself, homes shrouded in shadow.

"Hurry," she said. "I need to check the house."

"Is the kangaroo still following us?"

She glanced at the mirror. Only smoke and patches of green. "I don't know – if it is, it won't be too far behind."

"We'll go to the oval after – that's the assembly point, right?"

She opened her mouth to answer but stopped. "No. You should go to the river."

"What?"

"Behind the pub. It'll be safe."

"Not the oval?"

"It just feels right, okay?"

"And where are you going?"

"Yarsdale."

"Don't be stupid."

"I have to try."

The radio continued to hiss and buzz but she left it on, just in case something useful came through. Buildings loomed as Robert pulled the ute into the main street, each home or shopfront tinted crimson in the new darkness. People were loading baskets and tossing belongings into cars – those few that remained. A small boy tugged on the lead of a Jack Russell. Shops had been closed up – the Bakery's ever-present glowing sign for 'open' was dark. "Look, what if the road's cut off?" Robert said.

"I can't just leave him there – who knows how close the fire is?"

"It's close to us, that's how close it is. And the hospital will be the first place evacuated if it comes to that."

"What if something goes wrong?"

He waved a hand at the radio as he turned into a back street. "Check."

She fiddled with the tuning but nothing was clear. The broadcast seemed to be running through areas to the west. By the time they'd checked on Robert's place and he'd returned from inside with a photo album and a computer the day had darkened further. Ash lay heavy in the air, coating her tongue it seemed.

"Do we even have time for my place?" she called over the wind. It was almost hot enough to dry the sweat as it formed. The inside of the ute was littered with black and grey flecks of ash.

"We'll try."

Chambers Street was empty – a pram lay overturned in a front yard and Mrs Anderson's screen door rattled in the wind. A film of ash coated the front step when Lisa burst inside, kicking at boots in the hall as she dashed for her own laptop. In the study she snatched a photo of her and Mum and Dad from the wall – and one of Dad's paintings – the lone tree. God, would anything be left if the fire hit?

Robert beeped the horn.

Wait! She grabbed a paintbrush and dashed from the house and into the ute. "Go."

Wheels spun as Robert tore down the empty streets. "Still want to try the pub?"

"After I make sure Dad is all right."

"You don't know if the road is open."

"I'll drive myself if you want to stay."

"I don't think –"

"Robert, he's all I've got."

He shook his head but turned the car toward the rickety wooden Welcome sign instead of the river. Smoke still swirled between houses and electricity poles became slender sentries where they loomed from the heavy haze. Hot wind continued to buffet the vehicle. Her throat was still sore, despite them finishing off the water bottle. Even if the ute didn't have a broken window, smoke would have crept through the air vents, through every gap.

The road out of town started its gentle incline. Yet they'd barely been on it for a minute when Robert slowed at a huge, dark shape ahead. "What's this?" A long wall of steel resolved from the smoke and Robert stopped the ute.

A truck had jack-knifed. The same log truck that had flown down the hill before Jennings Lane. It blocked the road completely. "There's no way around," Robert said. The cab lay twisted on the edge of a steep slope leading down into the trees and the trailer covered the road, logs spilled like a hideous, giant game of Pick Up Sticks.

Dad.

There was no way to reach him now.

Chapter 26.

Lisa kicked a tyre. "God damn it."

The back roads to Yarsdale were a serious detour, several of which were in a direct path of the fire – and closer to the front than Lidelson itself. Maybe if she rang the hospital... She tried her mobile but the service didn't hold up. The towers were probably jammed. Or burnt to ash.

"Help me check on the driver," Robert called.

She ran forward, vaulting a log and grabbing hold of the trailer as she slid down torn earth beside the road. It wasn't a deathly plunge down to the trees, but if she slipped and started rolling, she'd break something. The truck's cab lay tucked into the trailer and this close, the scent of burnt rubber was strong even beneath the smoke.

"Hello? Are you all right?"

She climbed up the grated step and wrenched open the cabin door. A man in a flannelette shirt lay slumped over the wheel. He didn't move. She touched his shoulder and he groaned. Thank God – he had a chance. If he could walk.

And if the fire didn't sweep down on all of them.

"Hey, can you move?"

Another groan.

She leant out of the cab. Robert stood below. "He's alive. I'll try get him out." She wriggled closer to the driver. "What's your name?"

He blinked, finally focusing on her. "Ted." He lifted himself up and Lisa helped him lay back in the seat. He closed his eyes. A large bruise covered his forehead, the skin split. "Something jumped out. Tried to swerve."

"Don't worry about it now."

Robert climbed up beside her. "We need to lift him out and get somewhere safe."

"The river," Lisa said. "Can you walk?" she asked the driver.

"Don't know."

"Well, we're going to help. Ready?"

Robert climbed back down and the driver nodded and used the edge of the door to pull himself forward. Lisa took some of his weight, helping the man down to Robert, who caught him with a grunt.

"Sorry," Ted mumbled.

Lisa jumped down after and together the three navigated the slope, moving carefully with Robert on the lowest point. Ted's foot slipped but Lisa caught his arm. The paintbrush in her pocket dug into her leg as she strained, but together with Robert, they half-pulled, half-pushed Ted to the level stretch of road.

Without much room in the ute, Lisa helped Ted into the passenger seat. "I'll ride in the tray," she said. She climbed up over the dented part of the ute and gripped the roll bar.

Flecks of glowing red winked across the top of the cab

– embers. She spun. Red and black embers floated on the wind. The front was closing in.

"Go!" she shouted and thumped the roof.

Robert charged back into town. The embers flared and she squinted against the smoke. In the distance glowed more red spots, close to the ground, between buildings and beyond them – everywhere it seemed. New smoke rose in random patterns. Spot fires. The fire front was as little as a handful of kilometres away.

Even the spot fires would be enough trouble on their own. Anyone staying behind to try and defend their homes would have their hands full. As would the CFA – if they could even access the place. The crash wouldn't make it easy for the fire-trucks. Water-bombing might be possible but would it make a difference? How many homes would be lost? Lives?

Would the wind change?

Robert pulled up to the gravel car park before the pub's concrete steps. Only Bruce's old van was parked nearby. Lisa leapt down and helped Ted out. His colour was a little off but he seemed better able to walk. She got him up the steps and glanced back. Robert had one rifle in hand, the other over a shoulder and the laptops and photos in his free arm as he followed.

"We'll be safe in here," she told the truck driver as she thumped on the door.

Bruce came around the side of the pub. He wore a heavy-duty looking tank strapped to his back, a hose in one hand. A hammer hung from a tool belt. His sleeves were long and he wore a wide-brimmed hat. She could have laughed – he looked like a cross between Indiana Jones and an exterminator.

He blinked. "Lisa? Robert?" He rushed over. "Come inside."

The bar was empty – only one light glowed over the mirror, a chunky Dolphin torch standing upright. Stools and tables were darker shapes in the dim room. Even in here, a haze of smoke was perceptible. Smoke always found a way. Lisa got Ted to a chair and sat him down. "I'll find you some water," she said.

"Thanks."

Lisa ran around the bar and found a glass. The sinks were both full, as were buckets sitting on the counter. Piles of towels – the same towels she'd run through the washing machine enough times to know the individual marks and tears – sat nearby, ready to be soaked and lain across doorways and windows.

She filled the glass and took it to Ted, joining Robert and Bruce who were discussing the defence.

"I sent Pearl and the kids to her mum's. Matt's looking after his place in Yarsdale but I can't leave this old bastard." He slapped a wall. "Got me gutters full and the pump is sucking half the river onto the back yard. I've already soaked the verandah. Had the sprinklers running since last night but there's a lot of doors and windows to look after in here."

"We'll help," Robert told him.

"You sure? What about your place?"

Robert shook his head, his expression tight. "Insurance will cover anything that happens."

"Maybe you won't need it, right?"

His smile was a quick one. "Hope so."

"You can start with the ladder – I want to be able to get

at the ceiling if it catches fire."

Robert nodded and headed toward the pool room.

"Your dad okay, then?" Bruce asked.

"I don't know. I haven't been able to get through to the hospital."

"Keep yourself busy." He patted her arm, his glove damp. "Start soaking towels and finish lining the doors and windows. I'm off to check on the pump."

"Right." She glanced over at Ted, who seemed happy to simply sit with his head in his hands, then grabbed her first towel. She shoved it into a sink and ran to a blacked out window, lining it as best she could. The towel clumped in the sill, water dripping down the wall.

Outside, the wind raged on. Was the roar growing? How close was the fire? She needed to see. Damn it. Her heart started to thump – like it was trying to punch through her ribs. How bad was it going to get? They could all die. Would she even feel it? Or would the smoke get her first?

"Shit." She snatched another towel from the bench and kept going.

Robert soon joined her. When they emptied the sink, she refilled it and when they ran out of towels she snatched more from the linen closet. And once they were done, she started on bed sheets.

"Take the guest rooms," she shouted to Robert. "Use the laundry sink."

"Right."

Breathing hard, she took her dripping sheet to the back door that permitted access to the verandah and the outdoor setting which led toward the river. She glanced outside. One of Bruce's sprinklers spun, soaking the deck. The furniture and barbeque and its gas bottle had been removed and the shade cloth packed away somewhere.

The water in the river flowed on, the red sky reflected on the surface. Bruce was a little distance away, bent over a forty-four gallon drum, which had been cut in half, so as to cover the water pump.

She slapped the sheet down, spreading it along the floor. Her arms were aching but already their efforts were making a difference to the interior of the room. Less smoke seeped in – save for the front door and its yellow-frosted glass. No point doing that one yet.

How long until the fire-front hit?

"Robert?" She tried again, raising her voice. "Robert?"

He appeared from a hallway. "All done?"

"Yeah. I'm going to get Bruce inside."

"Good luck."

Heat blasted her when she opened the door. It stung her face and the skin of her hands – it even singed her eyeballs, or so it seemed. She squinted as her eyes watered. Beyond the ute, Bruce was spraying a small fire that had leapt up in the garden bed running along the fence. The trees had been cut back – she hadn't noticed before – no branches near windows or roof now.

And no hint of his usual clumsiness either; he was all purposeful movements.

But it was too late for that now. He had to get inside – right away. Smoke and fire raged across the town. Grass, building, tree – nothing was immune; fire climbed and blackened everything in its path. She ran down the steps, shouting. Bruce continued to douse the flames.

She caught his shoulder. "Bruce, it's too dangerous."

Could he hear?

He did. He stopped to glance at flames bursting from the windows of houses across the way, then nodded. They ran back to the pub, Bruce slamming the door shut. She took a heap of pillow cases from a nearby bucket and dumped them with wet slaps on the floor before the entry.

"Keep checking that the others are wet," Bruce shouted. "There's another torch in the hall too."

She leant against the sink to catch her breath. Had they done enough? There was no way to know until the front hit. "How long will it last?"

"Five minutes, maybe more, I'm guessing. It's a big one."

"Bigger than Black Saturday?" She'd been overseas – and lucky – to miss it.

"They say it's not but I think it's bad enough, isn't it?" He removed his hat and wiped his brow. "Choose a room and take some buckets with you too, Lisa. We can't let the fire catch hold. If things get bad, come back to the bar."

"I will."

He strode off and she flicked the torch on, illuminating smoke where it hovered in the passage, and took her bucket and began dousing the towels again. With the sink running she checked on Ted, who was asleep – his breathing slow and even. For now, she'd leave him to rest.

The roar outside built. Light darkened beyond the window shields; even the aluminium looked like it was searing hot. The very walls seemed to shudder. Lisa fell back and from somewhere in the pub, Robert shouted.

"It's going to hit!"

"In here," Lisa shouted back.

They rushed into the barroom. Walls continued to vibrate

with the force of the fire-front and she dashed back to the laundry to re-fill the bucket, only to leave it by the guest room door when more cries came from the bar. She sprinted back. Ted was coughing and shouting as smoke poured in from the pool room.

It was curling down from the manhole above the ladder.

"Oh God." How were they going to survive?

She snatched a pillowcase from the bar and soaked it in the sink, tying it over her mouth and nose. She took another bucket and climbed the ladder, squinting through the smoke and blinking against pummelling heat. Was her mouthguard dry already? Through the tears she could make out wobbly splashes of flame glowing in the ceiling – too far for her to reach.

"How bad is it?" Robert shouted. He had the ladder in his grip, his own face covered.

"It's above the bar itself but I can't get to it without climbing up. It's about a thousand degrees," she said.

"Bruce!" Robert cried.

The publican rushed into the room. He glanced at the roof. "Where is it?"

"Over the bar."

"Get the axe," he said, un-slinging his tank and pointing behind the bar. He hauled the tank over to a tap and started to re-fill it. "And any other buckets."

"You're going to break through from below?" she asked as Robert ran for the storeroom.

"Can't climb up there."

When Robert returned, he hopped up onto the bar and glanced back at her. "Here?"

She waved him further along. "Hurry."

He swung at the ceiling, hacking through the plaster. White crumbled around him, filling the haze as he swung again and again. His blows were a little slower than if he'd been swinging downwards, but fire gleamed in the ceiling when he broke through. Bruce shot his hose at the hole, causing more hissing steam. The fire-front outside was a roaring beast, seeming almost angry at their attempts to stop it devouring the pub and those inside.

Robert kept hacking at the roof, exposing beams and flaming insulation. When he fell back it was to switch axe for bucket – handed to him by Ted. He cast the water into the ceiling then called for another. Bruce was still hosing it down.

Some of the flames had escaped.

"Towards me," she shouted.

Bruce climbed up beside Robert and changed direction of his hose, the water soon dousing the new flames. "I'll keep an eye on this," he said. He wasn't shouting as loud as before. "Check the rest."

She climbed down and headed for the guest rooms where she paused. It was quieter outside. No more roaring, just a crackling from beyond the walls.

Had the front passed? Already?

Was it safe? She charged back to the bar and tested the front door handle with part of the towel, whipping her hand back as the heat stung through the fabric. Idiot.

"Lisa?" Bruce paused in his work.

"The front's passed – can't you hear it?"

"Be careful, don't rush."

She tried again, re-arranging the towel, and turned the handle to pull it open slowly, a wave of heat rushing over her skin. Beyond waited blackened land. The edges of flame curled around the garden and nearby properties. If they could put out the fires left after the front had passed, maybe they could save the pub.

Beyond the blasted earth lay other blazes and columns of smoke – charred houses as far as she could see. Chambers Street was too distant and cloaked in smoke to know whether her house had survived. The homes she could see were skeletons, twisted heaps of smouldering tin – or in some cases – smoke-scorched but still standing, often surrounded by wreckage of rooves, fences or cars. Powerlines had fallen into tangled piles; everywhere there was black, black, black.

Sirens screamed in the distance and she exhaled a shuddering breath that scratched at her throat.

"Bruce."

He joined her.

Tears poured down her cheeks. "We have to put out the smaller fires. We have to check for embers."

He rested a gloved hand on her shoulder. "It'll be right now."

Chapter 27.

The pub was saved, but so much was lost.

Ronnie's bakery. Half the general store and others she couldn't even recognise. Dozens of homes, cars and things she'd never expected to see melted – like the red post box on the corner of the little park on Main Street, where she'd seen the white roo.

The oval had become a city of tents. CFA trucks rolled through the ash-choked road often – one allowed her to hop onto the back, dropping her at Chambers Street, seeing as the ute was ruined. People might have died but no-one would tell her. Or maybe they didn't know yet. She couldn't find Gerry or Karen or even Detective McConnell and her phone was flat. Instead, she dragged her aching feet up her street, stirring the char. Sweat mingled with ash on her skin beneath the clearing sky.

Mrs Anderson's house was a blackened stump.

Beside it smouldered a heap that had once been Lisa's home. Nothing standing – just twisted tin and charred wood and the hints of her possessions. She stopped at the very edge of the wreckage, tears stinging her eyes, smoke burning her throat anew.

Everything still stood right at her feet – within reach, but gone. She might as well have never owned a single thing. Clothes, books and paintings – right down to the cutlery Steph gave her as a housewarming present – her feather-top bed, the filing cabinet and the things Mum left behind. The little yellow scarf Lisa had never let herself wear – the one Mum bought with her first pay from her job at the corner store as a teenager.

"God damn it," she screamed.

Lisa kicked the rubble, again and again, letting out some of her rage before turning to run for Ronald Street. Her shoes kicked up more ash as she thundered down the road, leaping over a fallen street light and pumping her arms harder. When she reached the blackened sign for Ronald Street she slowed, breathing hard, but she smiled too.

Dad's house had survived.

Somehow, most of the street had avoided the onslaught of the fire front. Embers glowed on the concrete path at the empty house on the corner, but Dad's place was okay. She dashed into the yard and uncoiled the hose, prowling the yard for embers but found none at the limits of the hose.

She hosed the place down anyway, climbing up the fence to check the gutters.

A bucket was next, as she completed the full circuit of the yard. Nothing was amiss...still. Sticking around wouldn't hurt. All it would take would be a wind change and something might flare up.

Inside, the house remained just as she left it, save for

the scent of ash. Only the radio was quiet and Dad wasn't in his chair. She moved into the kitchen and took a drink from the fridge, snapping the ring pull open on soft drink – creaming soda. She leant against the bench and sipped at it, paintbrush tightening her jeans pocket. Bubbles from the soft drink weren't all that soothing on her throat but it was cold. And the sugar hit...she needed it.

"What now?" she croaked.

The tap gave no answer. Nor the sink or the dish-rack or the tea-towel with its faded picture of The Big Pineapple. Robert would be salvaging his shop – it had partially survived. Bruce was keeping an eye on Ted and hopefully Gerry was safe; he'd be off helping someone somewhere. And Steph and Dave, had they left? Was their cafe okay? Were they okay?

She dragged herself to the phone and dialled Yarsdale Hospital.

Come on, work. Work.

No dial tone.

Were the lines cut? If the fire moved west in a zig-zag instead of continuing south, Yarsdale would be in trouble.

Maybe if she tried again in a little while. She completed another circuit of the house before heading back inside to call the hospital again – but no luck. Next, she called Steph's mobile – network busy. Maybe heading back to the pub was the best choice. Bruce had a satellite phone somewhere too.

The oval was too chaotic.

She snorted.

Too chaotic. Yet, she wanted to be around people. Maybe just a few, rather than half the town. She locked up and headed out, checking on the house and the neighbouring properties one last time, then crossing the street. No-one around. Like a ghost town. A faint wind stirred, curling little black tornadoes that soon dissolved. She kicked at the ash, scuffing black marks along the paler bitumen.

At a stronger gust she turned away – and froze.

The bloody kangaroo waited at the end of the street. It merely stood, watching her. Too distant to be sure; but its skin and fur seemed darker. Burnt. Yet it was upright. Was it Ben driving the body into the streets? Or, the roo itself? Was there even anything left of Ben inside? Had there *ever* been anything of him in there? Was it simply feral? No. Stupid. It was beyond feral. More than human, more than animal.

Whatever. Didn't matter. Not anymore. Just...why couldn't it leave her alone?

"What do you want?" she called.

No answer.

Lisa crossed to the side of the street and the roo moved, keeping a parallel course. It matched her speed when she broke into a swift walk, angling closer. With little in the way of cover, she couldn't hide and couldn't lose the creature either.

She picked up speed. The kangaroo matched her again. Maybe if she made a break for it when the roo entered the maze of half-standing homes, she could reach the pub. Maybe. If nothing else, she'd have shelter – and one of the guns – hadn't Robert brought them inside?

At an intersection, with the pub's dark-tiled roof in sight, Lisa broke into a sprint.

The kangaroo leapt into the first yard, crashing through the blackened walls. Lisa's chest burned as she ran. Glancing back once, she saw the roo burst from the thin frame of the last house, flinging charred planks and beams into the air.

She pushed through the wobbling in her limbs but she was already slowing. Too long awake, too long tense, too long fighting the fire – she was stuffed. She stumbled down to a jog. The thump of the kangaroo neared. Somehow, she crossed the road and began to climb the driveway, sooty shoes crunching on gravel and then concrete. Lisa turned halfway-up; the roo bore down on her.

She screamed as it leapt but fell into a crouch, slipping down the steps.

The roo crashed into the cement above her. It cracked the stair. She scrambled back, edging toward the side of the pub. Ben – or the kangaroo – whatever it was, stepped down one at a time. An awkward, unnatural movement that only made it more terrifying. She continued her slow retreat, the beast stalking her. Where it stepped, smudges of blood and charred skin remained behind. The chest heaved, glimpses of pink visible through the fur. An ear had melted down to a stub and blood trailed from the mouth. One arm looked a little longer than the other, its claw stunted. How was it alive? How was it staying together? A huge tear exposed muscles in its leg; amazing that it could still hop.

Did flesh wobble? Bone even peeked through one shoulder. And yet, its eyes blazed with some rage, some conflict. The claws might be battered but they would still kill her if she was careless.

On she walked, never taking her eyes off the creature.

She waved a hand behind her, navigating still-warm posts and stump-like shrubs until she drew level with the blackened decking of the verandah and then down the lawn, stumbling over the melted end of the pump's hose, down the sloping grass – every blade now nothing more than a crunching corpse of char.

Until a small fence stopped her at the water's edge.

Ash floated down the river, choking it, muting even the sparkling sun it tried to reflect.

The roo followed.

She knew what to do.

The water.

The vision – the white kangaroo hadn't meant for the river as a place of refuge, but something else. As a weapon – hadn't she? Lisa stepped over the fence and splashed into the shallows.

"Follow if you want me," she said.

The kangaroo shuddered. Its jaws snapped as it leapt. She fell into the sluggish current as water exploded in a grey wall. The roo burst forward, jaws agape but she twisted. Its body crashed into her, a powerful forearm swiping down at her leg. She cried out but caught the roo by the neck, dragging it into the water.

It had to work.

She clung to the neck, the roo's head falling over her shoulder to gnash at her back but never connecting with flesh. The deeper they went the looser the body beneath her became. She hauled at the huge weight. Dark flakes filled the water, blood blackening the sludge as the red kangaroo disintegrated – pulled apart by the mild current.

As if it had never truly been connected.

The kangaroo began to shudder. She pushed on the body, fingers sliding through flesh and hitting bone. The spine came free, hooked over her shoulder, with the roo's head acting like an anchor. She dragged it through the water as

she spun, trying to keep her own head above the surface –
the river growing deeper as the current tugged her further
from the pub.

Toes scraped the sandy bottom.

Was the roo finished?

Lisa gripped the head, whose flesh was running, melting.
A greasy sensation coated her hands and she shuddered as a
yellowed, ancient skull was revealed. The basement! Before it
dissolved completely, one of the eyes blinked. And it wasn't
Ben's eye but a black orb, a black mirror. In it stood a blonde
girl, alone where she waited beneath a lamppost in a pale
wasteland, blushes of yellow in the earth. A wind twirled
her hair.

Then nothing.

The old bone dragged her down – suddenly heavy
beyond its size. Her head slipped beneath the surface and
she released the skull, thrashing up toward air.

Something held her back.

She kicked but the spine had curled around her leg. It
drew her deeper. Her heart thumped as she fought the tangle.
No! She bent in the darkness, fingers finding vertebrae,
giving them a jerk with both hands. The bones fell apart
with a muted 'click' that should have been difficult to hear.

Her lungs burnt. She slashed at the water with her limbs,
heading for the wavering glow of the surface.

And broke with a gasp.

Sunlight and air surrounded her as she drifted
downstream, spluttering. Nearby, the skull surfaced. It was
being borne away but seemed to face her; independent of
the swirls in the water. Worse, it refused to sink, somehow
the skull stayed afloat as it drifted. A light flickered in the

sockets and then it slipped around a bend in the river.

Gone.

Her head slipped under again; she'd stopped treading to watch the skull. Bursting free once more, she swam for the shore, closing her mouth to the ash-clogged water that splashed around her strokes.

Heaving herself up the bank to clamber onto the grass, she lay on her back. Her arms and legs – it was transmutation, they were lumps of lead! She breathed in, air rasping as high above, the contrail of a jet streaked across a blue sky now free of smoke.

Who was the girl?

Why did the kangaroo want her to see it?

And was Ben truly gone? Had he saved her in that first encounter, or had he driven a kangaroo to madness? It was just as possible that the skull devoured Ben. If so, where was it now?

She closed her eyes. Most likely she'd never know the truth.

And maybe it didn't matter anymore.

Chapter 28.

Detective McConnell strode into the pub, his face smudged with ash. Lisa waved for him to join her at one of the tables she'd managed to collapse into. Her jeans still dripped into the puddle on the floor. Bruce was no-where to be seen. Knowing him, he'd be helping others, now that his old pub was safe. She'd have to mop the floor for him later.

She crushed a cigarette butt into a tray.

"Glad to see you're alive," he said as he sat. It was almost satisfying to see soot covering his face, hands and shirt. A weariness lined his features, deep beneath the skin – he was human after all.

"I wish I had something clever to say but yeah, me too."

He chuckled. "But you're not glad to see me safe?"

"Depends on whether you're still hell-bent on arresting me for murder."

"Murders."

"And?"

"I've decided something," he said with a long sigh. "I'll

never know exactly what's gone on here."

She glanced over his shoulder to the river. "Me either."

"Did you feel like a swim?"

"Yeah."

"Are you all right?"

Impossible to know the answer to that. "Just worried about Dad."

"If you can help me one more time, we'll go see him."

"What about the jack-knifed truck?"

"SES cut a path." He stood. "I hear that the hospital is fine and that the patients are being returned. What do you think?"

She exhaled. Tension flowed from her shoulders as they slumped. Finally, some good news. If Dad had been hurt... "Thank you. What do you need?"

"I want to meet Gerry out at the Drummond's residence."

"Why?"

"We've found something that doesn't make sense. Could use your opinion again."

"Now? What about the town?"

"Best to let the folks who know what they're doing handle that. And this won't take too long."

"All right." Lisa followed him to the silver sedan, shoes squelching at every step. "Sorry about this," she said. "It's going to ruin your car seat."

"Don't worry – my side is all ash and dirt."

He set off at a fair clip, engine humming. Trees lining the road were burnt, some to cinders. In others, red embers glowed from within black husks like slitted, evil eyes. CFA volunteers in their yellow gear spread along the roadside, hunting for embers.

"Is everyone okay?" she asked.

"Mostly. Lots of livestock is gone – Healy's sheep farm was hit bad. And Lidelson lost two residents to the fire. Gerry knows their names, I can't remember right now, sorry."

"Oh." Who? Once again, the unfairness of life.

He hesitated. "There is one question I want to ask you. I can't promise anything, Lisa, but I'll say this much – I don't think you're a killer."

"Thank you." She glanced at him. He drove with his eyes on the road, hands at the perfect 'ten' and 'two' positions on the wheel. "What did you want to ask?"

"Do you think Ben Drummond killed his friends?"

Not the question she'd expected... "Why?"

He sighed again, weariness clear. "I'm getting ahead of myself. It's probably easier to show you."

The Drummond property was damaged but not in ruin. Burnt grass crossed the fences and one entire side of the house was blackened. Somehow, the owl had survived. A police cruiser waited in the driveway and McConnell parked beside it.

"He'll be round back."

More blackened earth in the backyard, shrubs burnt down to charcoal.

Gerry rose from a hole in the earth, resting a hand on a shovel. Smudged with ash and trails of sweat, his face brightened when he saw her. "Lisa!"

Her heart gave a little flip at the sight of him and before she knew what she was doing, she ran over and he crushed her into his chest then set her down. "You're all right."

"You too." She smiled up at him.

"All right, children," McConnell said. "Let's see to

business, you can have a proper reunion later."

Lisa flushed, then looked away. Why was she blushing? Shit, it was like high school all of a sudden. There was no reason to blush, was there? She was just relieved to actually see him, to know he was okay. She'd known him since school. And maybe she hadn't been able to figure it out for herself right away – but she was safe with him. There were no hidden motives with Gerry. No games. He was who he appeared to be.

Which was a wonderful thing.

But right now was the wrong time for all that. Help McConnell then check on Dad. Figure out exactly what she was feeling later.

"We found these." Gerry gestured to the ground beside the hole, where a set of claws rested. Covered in soil, they looked to have been hacked off. He stepped aside. Beyond him, dozens more holes. And more claws, of varying sizes. Bones too. She moved forward. Kangaroo. Kangaroo. Wallaby. Goanna – even Koala. Each next to a hole. "Some were buried quite shallow. Others we found half-melted in the garden, as if they'd been stashed," Gerry continued.

"What do you think?" McConnell asked.

She frowned. Why? Wait – the boneyard. That had to be it. Many of the bodies had been missing claws. Even one of the roos dumped in her yard was missing one. But why had Ben needed them? Why did he make his own boneyard here? Some of the bones looked pretty old. "I think it doesn't make sense," she said.

The Detective nodded. "It would seem that not only is your ex a prolific shooter, but he is also quite disturbed. In any event, it would match your statement about what Mr

Lindgren said to you, about Ben being crazy. It would also be consistent with the wounds on most of the bodies. We'll be testing the claws we recover to that end. It's likely he'd been using them to conceal his activities."

"Consistent except for Fathead," Lisa said. She nearly kicked herself with her wet boots. Don't cast doubt, let McConnell go down that path. No matter that what he'd find would be a lie – it was probably the best way to resolve things in a manner that would make sense. From a law-enforcement standpoint, anyway.

And it just might keep her out of jail.

"Maybe it was somehow more personal with James. I doubt we'll know unless Mr Drummond turns up. We've received word from his parents – they are overseas." He walked the lines of bones, scribbling on his pad. "And they haven't heard from him and are understandably upset. I'd like to have your thoughts on that. You had frequent contact with him of late."

Thank God Jennifer and Paul were alive. "Last I saw him was when I came here to warn him. About the murders."

"And?"

"He didn't care. He wasn't worried at all. Can't we test that skin?"

"Once things calm down," McConnell said. "And he indicated nothing to you about his intentions?"

She shrugged. "He boasted about a rifle. He probably went hunting again and got caught in the fire." Not exactly a lie.

McConnell noted her answer in his pad. "Could be."

"I could believe he got caught up there somewhere," Gerry said, turning a half-circle to gaze at the blackened bush. The scent of char was still thick in the air.

"Probably right," McConnell said. He exhaled heavily then flipped his book closed. "We might head to Yarsdale then. Gerry, keep cataloguing these."

"Will do." Gerry looked to Lisa. "Tell me how your dad is going?"

She smiled. "I will."

Back on the road, McConnell tried the radio but reception was still uneven. He turned it down. "Do you have a place to stay? I drove by Chambers Street looking for you."

"Dad's."

He cleared his throat. "Glad to hear his place survived."

"How is your mum?"

"Safe, luckily."

"Good."

They spoke little on the rest of the journey, until the Yarsdale hospital appeared, unscathed atop the hill. Most of the town was free of fire-damage. Smoke still hung in the air like half-visible poison, hanging over the lawns beneath the hospital and in the car park.

"Outlying homes were lost here but it's nothing like Lidelson," Detective McConnell said as he walked her to the sliding doors.

"Unlucky," she murmured. His words were like faint radio signals.

They headed down the clean corridors and at a small cafeteria, McConnell stopped. "I'll be here when you're ready," he said.

She nodded and walked on.

At the station a tiny nurse took her to see him. "He's pretty good today. Pretty annoyed at all the 'fuss' as he called it."

Lisa smiled at the nurse as the woman left then took a breath. She pulled open the curtain and there he was, pacing beside his bed, staring up at the television mounted to the roof. Good colour in his cheeks and he was moving pretty well. He'd even shaved and, it seemed, someone had found him some English Leather. Sunlight lanced in from between the curtains, splashing across the bed.

She nearly cried out 'Dad' but his eyes stopped her.

Her heart twisted.

Not again.

"Hello, Mr Thomas." She summoned a smile from a happier time – whenever that had been.

"Hello?" He squinted at her. "Do we know each other?"

"Yes, I've...visited before," she said.

"I see." He grinned. "So, you swam here, did ya?"

She had to smile back, even though it hurt. That humour was all Dad – part of him was still there. "I fell in a river."

"Sounds like a good story – why don't you tell me about it?"

"I'd love to but it's a long one. And the nurse didn't want me here long after the evacuation."

He snorted. "What a lot of rubbish that was. Nothing happened!"

"Well, what if I made a start today and came back tomorrow?"

"Good idea – and a lovely young woman like you? Be a nice change from all the grumpy nurses."

"They don't seem that bad."

"You don't have to put up with them," he whispered – quite loudly.

Lisa laughed and sat next to the bed. Something dug into her leg, through the jeans, and she pulled free two halves of her big paintbrush. How had it survived everything?

Her dad smacked his head. "I remember."

She straightened. "You do?"

"You visited before. We talked about painting."

"We did." Better than nothing. And he was still smiling. Not the absent-minded smile she'd grown accustomed to or the uncertain smile when he couldn't remember something. "I brought it for you, actually. In case they might let you do some painting?"

"Well, isn't that thoughtful. Thank you." He raised an eyebrow. "Did you bring two halves of a canvas too?"

He drew another laugh from her. This was the dad she remembered; if only he'd remember her. "I guess it snapped when I fell in the river."

"Well, not to worry. Look." He gestured to his bedside table and a sketchpad atop it. "I sketched one of my dreams, you know. They gave me some pencils."

Lisa opened the pad.

A beautiful white kangaroo stood on the page. It loomed out of darkness where her father had used the lead to smudge shadows. Her fur was drawn in thin strokes, light enough to suggest the ruffling of a faint breeze. Her tail curled into the dark; she was poised at the point of flight, as if she might leap off the page at any moment. Yet the brightness of the roo's eyes could not entirely conceal a sadness and another figure lurked in the shadow – more impression than form, eyes narrowed, jaw agape.

The red roo.

Lisa shivered.

A hand covered her own. "So, let's start this tale of yours," Dad said. "How did you fall in then?"

She smiled through the tears.

Acknowledgements

As ever, I want to start by thanking my wife Brooke, who urges me to do better and who saves all my first drafts from being trainwrecks!

I need to express thanks also to Wildlife Victoria, the awesome volunteers at my local CFA station and VicRoads. As with my last work, I want to credit them with the accuracies and take responsibility myself for any faults in the research. Certainly thank you to the Alchemists (CJ, Tess & Rebekah) whose input is inexhaustible and to the many readers and writers who also helped me: Aderyn, Kerry, Lynn, Gary, AJ, HL, and Eliza, but also Catherine and Jen too, thank you each!

Once again, endless gratitude is due to Amanda J Spedding for taking the story beyond what I thought possible and also to David Schembri for patience and assistance when it came to formatting the ebook.

A special thanks also to Louis at Indigo Forest Designs for such a brilliant cover and for stepping in at short notice!

Ashley

About Ashley

Ashley is a poet, novelist and teacher living in Australia
Aside from reading and writing, he loves volleyball, Studio
Ghibli and *Magnum PI*, easily one of the greatest television
shows ever made.

You can find him online at @Ash_Capes or on his fiction
blog, *www.cityofmasks.com* and at *www.ashleycapes.com* for
poetry, where you can also sign up to his newsletter for
competitions, giveaways and sneak peeks of forthcoming
titles.

Also by Ashley Capes

Fiction

The Fairy Wren
A Whisper of Leaves

The Bone Mask Trilogy
1. *City of Masks*
2. *The Lost Mask*
3. *Greatmask (forthcoming)*

Poetry

pollen and the storm
stepping over seasons
orion tips the saucepan
between giants
old stone
7 Years